Advance Praise for
The Slow Midnight on Cypress Avenue

"Consistently captivating audiences with his youthful dynamism and sincerity, Mike is a natural writer and poet, and everyone who has ever read his work or heard him read it himself knows it."

— David Amram, Famed Classical Composer, Conductor, and Multi-instrumentalist

"I spent five seasons in Queens, NY, prowling center field of Shea Stadium. Mike Figliola captures the heartbeat of NYC better than any book I know."

— Lenny Dykstra, *New York Times* Bestselling Author of *House of Nails*

"Mike Figliola's debut novel *The Slow Midnight on Cypress Avenue* is the untapped prose of both people and place rarely given life in the way newcomer Figliola has accomplished. The relationships between the characters are so tangible you can almost sense their presence rise up from the pages, centered around the life of a veteran whose all-seeing eyes on his front stoop help intertwine this story of humanity, horror, aspiration, loss, and hope."

— Salena Zito, Author, *The Great Revolt* and national political reporter for the *Washington Examiner* and *NY Post*

"It's been over a decade since Mike Figliola was my producer on WOR's hit show *Food Talk*, but his daily witticisms, brilliant storytelling, and creative genius are as fresh a memory as my first day of school. *The Slow Midnight on Cypress Avenue* is the happy benefactor of Mike's years of toil as a writer. It's set in a reluctant neighborhood in Queens, New York, and features characters and stories only found in a Manhattan-adjacent 'hood like Ridgewood. Part magic, part audacious, and always impossible to believe, Mr. Figliola keeps it very interesting on Cypress Avenue."

> — Rocco Dispirito, James Beard Award-winning celebrity chef and Author of *Rocco's Keto Comfort Food Diet: Eat the Foods You Miss and Still Lose Up to a Pound a Day*

"Only a real Queens guy could ever have written this book. It oozes authenticity: the larger-than-life characters and egos, the gruff spoken word poetry of the dialogue, the world-weary swagger, the A train, the dope and the booze—there's just no faking this stuff. Filled with humor and heartbreak, Figs makes you feel like you're actually part of a neighborhood where nothing comes easy but beauty abounds in gritty everyday reality."

> — Elie Honig, CNN Legal Analyst and former federal prosecutor

the
slow midnight
on
cypress avenue

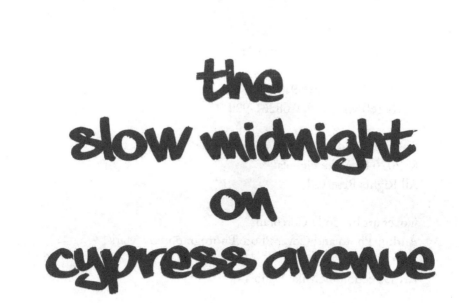

the slow midnight on cypress avenue

MIKE FIGLIOLA

PERMUTED
PRESS

A PERMUTED PRESS BOOK

ISBN: 978-1-68261-919-3
ISBN (eBook): 978-1-68261-920-9

Cover art by Cody Corcoran
Author Photo and Cover Photo Photography by Mark
Zustovich
Art Direction by Mike Figliola

PERMUTED
PRESS

Permuted Press, LLC
New York • Nashville
permutedpress.com

Published in the United States of America

CONTENTS

book i: morning

book ii: afternoon

book iii: night

BOOK 1

PART 1

Mr. Jean

i checked my watch. It was quarter past eight in the morning; another Sunday on Cypress Avenue.

"Dezzy! Dezzy baby! Bring me some wine. And the radio! The portable radio on my bookshelf. Also my reading glasses and if you can find it, a *Weekly World News* paper, one of the old ones I have stashed next to my couch in the wicker basket. The one with Bat Boy and Elvis on the cover."

I turned and looked straight up at my apartment window. It was closed with the drapes drawn.

Surely she will hear me.

No response. Just a long dead silence. Dezzy's usual horseshit.

"Dezzy honey, did you hear me? I need my portable radio—on the bookshelf. Also the reading glasses and the *Weekly World News* with Bat Boy and Elvis. And wine, just a cup or two—oh, just bring the bottle. Thank you honey, I am on the stoop!"

The wind kicked up a little. Smelled like rain. Hot summer rain. Not the cleansing kind. It was a typical sort of rain that readily fell over Ridgewood.

"Sam, the window is closed, she can't hear you. Why don't you get the stuff yourself?"

"Dezzy—Dezzy baby!"

"Would you stop yelling? It's eight o'clock in the morning!" I knew that voice. It was Fran; fat old Fran. She spent her time preaching to the people in this neighborhood almost as much as the southern pastor at St. Aloysius Church.

"And people are on their way to church too, Samuel, for goodness' sakes!"

Fran was the superintendent of our apartment building. The role had gone to her fat head and she wielded the broom with which she swept our hallway with an iron fist. She was one of the changeless and useless faces in the neighborhood. They were everywhere and usually I wouldn't respond to her or anyone. It was a waste of time. Fran was in luck, though; Dezzy wasn't awake yet and I had time to waste.

"It's almost eight thirty. They are all already at church. Why don't you mind your own business and go floss your false teeth?"

She ignored my insult and went on: "Plus, it's going to rain, you fool. And why don't *you* go inside and read your magazine and drink your wine and let that poor girl sleep. It's eight o'clock in the morning!"

"Bah! Dezzy! DEZZY!!!" I yelled louder this time, like Ralph Kramden yelling upstairs to Ed Norton. I never did quite sound like Ralph, though. I was a blowhard with no blow.

"Dezzy!!"

Still weak. My brother Harold had a little more growl when he reached down into his gut—a gut mostly full of scotch. His bark still fell short. Harold knew why. I told him regularly: there is never going to be another Jackie Gleason. That type of man is dead and buried. Harold would scoff and yell louder. No dice. I reminded Harold that Jackie Gleason was poor and unassuming as Ralph Kramden, but sad and corrupt as Maish Rennick; the "Great One" himself born and bred in Brooklyn just like us and only five miles or so from here. All that laughing and life, echoed into the walls and saturated into the streets, now paved and tarred over by time. Seems like forever ago, beyond yesteryear. Harold is dead now. I wish he weren't.

My brother Harold was born a day after I was, only a year later: July the ninth, 1945. I hate thinking about birthdays. Birth-deaths are more like it. It was me and Harold for as long as I can remember living in or around the six to eight family apartment buildings on Cypress Avenue. Our feet walked the half-paved/half-cobblestone streets in shoes that were stuffed with cardboard or two pair of socks when the holes got too big. We grew up in a hell that every other kid grew up in during the 1950s. That hell was put aside during long games of stickball in the middle of the street with an open Johnny pump firing onto our sunburned legs. We lived with my mother's sister Betty at the time. Harold and I never knew our mother and father. They disappeared when Harold and I were very small. They weren't married, which at the time was high treason in the middle of moral-majority America. I used to believe that my father had moved away into the Southwest to open a saloon with his brother. My aunt told us he wasn't worth his salt anyway, being that only an idiot would get himself killed after not paying a gambling debt. Aunt Betty knew all about gambling so I believed her. But she changed the story of how he died throughout the years, which pissed Harold off. One time she said my father wasn't even smart enough to make it to the Southwest and that he died with a rack of ribs in front of him somewhere near Kansas City. She also claimed he went to Mexico to become a cult leader and died after trying to convince a crowd he could walk on water. The stories of his departure usually came forth every year around the same time. Harold would stew. I would play stickball. That's how we dealt with all of that. My aunt told us our mother never recovered from him leaving. She sat us down on the sofa and lowered the TV volume to tell us, calling her death "onset rheumatic fever" or some horseshit like that. Harold and I knew better. My mother would drink fevers away with gin and Bromo-Seltzer. In reality she walked in front of an oncoming southbound train at Lexington and 51st Street. No mother of ours was going to go out with a damn fever. No, she died the way we wanted her to. I just wish she had done it a little later on, when Harold was stronger and had his footing.

A drop of rain touched down right in front of my foot and broke my daydream. It directly hit an ant that was slowly dragging a leaf behind it. Too bad. It got worse, though; the ant fell over onto its back and another couple of droplets almost washed it away into the street. Too bad. Now its leaf would be doubly heavy with rain water. Poor bastard. But Fat Fran was right about me having to go inside to read and drink. There I would be: inside that old railroad apartment, like a box, like a coffin, to read and be alone. Dead and buried.

"How many eight o'clock in the mornings do I have left, Fran? How many you give me? A year's worth? Two years' worth? I don't know, Fran, but did you notice that this could be my last summer—last time on the stoop to read, have wine, hear the birds and watch the ants—like this poor guy, struggle to pull a leaf to the nest and wham!—struck down by a droplet of rain. This could be it for me, you see? And all I wanted, Fran, was Dezzy to bring me my things so I didn't have to walk back up this damn stoop again!" I wanted to put Fat in front of the Fran every time I said it. But I would reserve that for indoors.

"Here you go, Mister Jean," said a soft, morning-cracked voice. Dezzy stood in the doorway of the apartment building holding the items I shouted for. She didn't look so good: her eyes were slits, and her hair was arranged in a poorly made ponytail; however, she was half-smiling at me with dimples placed in the middle of her cheeks by the Lord. "Is this all you wanted? Glasses, magazines, a radio, and wine?"

I smiled and looked at Fran as if to say, *You see? She cares about me. She heard me. Didn't matter what time it was, she was going to bring me what I asked her for.* I hated that fatty.

Fran shook her head and looked up to the sky. She was immediately splashed on the nose by an incoming raindrop.

"No, Dezzy, I want to come inside. It's going to rain. Can you help me in, baby? Good day, Fran." I smirked as Dezzy set aside my things and helped me back up the two cement stoop stairs and into the hallway.

"Goodbye, Samuel," Fran snipped. "And try to be a little quieter. It's eight o'clock in the morning after all."

Dezzy turned and waved to her. "Not a problem, Fran. I will take care of him and keep him quiet with wine and radios and whatever else he wants."

"Try to be a little less fat," I mumbled.

"What, Samuel?" asked Fran.

I said, "You see! That's the respect there. That can only be taught, Fran! Dezzy was raised well!" We closed the door behind us.

"I don't like talking to Fran, Dezzy," I whispered. "She may seem harmless—even inviting—but you can never be sure of what's underneath that muumuu she wears, you know?"

Dezzy laughed and swung her ponytail around. "There's nothing under that muumuu that is sinister, Mister Jean."

"Just fat."

"Fat is harmless."

Dezzy's eyes were opening now. They were bright, but they were supported by puffy black bags, markers that reminded me that she hadn't slept right in the three years since she told me her father passed away. Her father hadn't passed away in reality; he had left the family years ago. Dezzy mourned his leaving like a death. Her laugh and smile belied it. You would never know she had been worn down. Her full name was Desponda Ramona Rivera and she was born of a family full of internal warfare that lived a few apartment building doors down. That is all I knew. That is all I could handle.

"You are naïve sometimes, Dezzy."

"Naïve, Mister Jean?"

"Stop that 'Mister Jean' shit."

"Why? I like calling you Mister Jean; it fits your pipe and beer and easy chair."

"I am not smoking a pipe, sitting in my easy chair, or drinking beer right now, so cut it out."

A light fixture creaking above reminded me the ceiling fan was not installed properly. The blades spun wildly and loose, but they kept the entire apartment cool. And with the windows open at the start of a summer rain, the cross ventilation blew up any unsuspecting female visitor's dress. Dezzy never wore dresses. That was too bad.

"I just don't see how I am naïve. Religious people are naïve. Taxpayers are naïve. Those who hand out spare change to tramps hanging around subway stations and think that money isn't going directly to a wine bottle or a fully loaded syringe are naïve. I, Mister Jean, am none of that."

"Cut out the 'Mister Jean' shit," I said. "Besides, I know you are none of that. You are very smart—smart as a whip who no man could ever take advantage of. You are a strong and independent type of gal full of prolific, tested wisdoms and well thought-out plans not of the *Mice and Men* variety." I paused and pointed to the kitchen. "Now pour me some wine."

She blinked twice.

"You can pour yourself some, too—there's more than one clean glass in the cupboard."

"I know. I did the dishes for you this morning."

"That's a good girl. Thanks. Two ice cubes, please."

I walked over to the open window in the bedroom before she could blink or answer or anything else and placed both my hands firmly on the frame. The once-clean sheer linen white drapes, now yellowed with the passage of time and perfumed tobacco smoke that spilled out of my evening pipes, were blowing in and out of the window like beckoning arms—the enchanted arms of Mr. Death.

"Storm's almost here," I whispered to myself. I used to love day storms. The freshness of rain, the solitude it unassumingly provided to me, the peace I found inside with the lights off but the grey storm-cloud-filtered sunlight filling the room, and the subsequent nap that might come with it. Those days I was able to share such things with another woman. No "Mr. Jean" or a Fat Fran in a muumuu dress. Just good old Samuel Jean (friends called me Sam or Snap when we were playing pool in the halls that dotted the many miles that Myrtle Avenue spanned from Brooklyn to Queens). The pool hall would be filled with guys looking for a fight or just looking to lay down a few bucks for a cream soda and low wager. And I would greet them both.

Here's how it would go down:

I would stand at the foot of the table, sip the cream soda and scotch, slam down a few bills, match my good eye up to the green felt and aim my lucky stick at that white hot cue ball. The boys watched. The girls watched. The barkeep counted the day's keep with one eye and watched me out of his other. Outside the rain would be washing down, cooling the summer streets and streaking across the front glass of the pool hall. Juke roared Harlem-born jazz and bop in a never-ending loop. And at the other end of the table would stand a red-haired big-bosomed baby staring straight at me with an Alice Kramden smile. It was Goldie Samuels. She never wavered, just watched and waited for that cue ball to deliver a devastating blow to the boy's hopes on the table. She knew it would happen. She let them know by paying them no mind and waiting for me, for my shot, for my moment to sink that last striped billiard ball in the corner pocket, take the pot of cash, then deliver a dinner of steak, mash, and plenty of beer. The boys would yell "Come on, Snap! You ain't got it this time, Snap." But that is the last sound anyone would hear until my ball fired off the end of my cue stick and smacked straight into the others already deposited in that pocket. After a few handshakes, victory marches, and cocktails, we mad-dashed through the rain back to her apartment—a railroad on the edge of Fresh Pond Road and Myrtle—and crashed into her unmade Murphy bed. But before the broad stroke of lovemaking night, she'd stand up and fling wide open the window that faced the street—and the rain-born breeze would blow her hair and the soft drapes and her Bettie Page dress everywhere. We never did care.

And she never called me Mr. Jean.
A hand gently grabbed my shoulder.
"Here's your wine, Mister Jean."

I turned around, startled out of my yesteryear fantasy to see Dezzy with a glass in her hand. It was filled with wine and two ice cubes.

"Thank you, Dezzy. I think I'll have my pipe and go sit in my easy chair now."

a girl of little dreams

I wonder what makes old men sadder: the loss of a dog or the loss of their lady? Mr. Jean lost both between here and there over the years; at least I think he did. Now he is sad again, sitting in that easy chair, silent and alone. But I wonder if it's losing the wag of the dog's tail or the shake of his old woman's ass that saddens him more. Perhaps it is neither; perhaps it's the routine of it all. I can imagine Mr. Jean in those same pajamas day in and day out, taking pisses and craps and then cooking the same sardine-and-capers sandwich over a nonstick pan Fran bought for him one Christmas. Then me coming by, doing his dishes, hearing him call Fran fat until he gets sad again. But what was it? Was it about his dog or his lady? Who has time to figure such things out anyway?

"Okay, Mister Jean, I'm gonna get going. Enjoy your pipes and wines and magazines." No answer. No matter. I grab a handful of change sitting on the kitchen counter and leave through the front door, pull it closed, fix my bra, smell my breath in my hand, and sneak slowly down the stairs past Fran's apartment to the yellow-lit hallway. Thank god

no one is on the pay phone. The day is young. And so am I.
Pip is sure to be up now. I count the change out and place
the coins in the slot.

BRRRNG BRRRNG

"Hello."

"Pip, it's Dezzy."

"Same spot, hun?"

"How long?"

"Ten minutes."

"Don't make me wait too long."

"Ten freakin' minutes, I said."

"Can we go for a ride when you get here? I just want to
take a drive in the rain."

"Oh shit, it's raining? Be more like half hour now."

"What! Do you drive like Mister Magoo in the rain?"

"Who is Mister Magoo?"

"Forget it, something I heard someone say once. Means
you drive slow and dopey."

"Ten minutes. And yeah, we can go for a ride. Bye."

CLICK

He is learning. I never say bye when I hang up. That's
why Pip said it and didn't wait for me.

Ten minutes is a long damn time. Why do people take
so long to do things? Ten minutes. It's never ten minutes.
It's eighteen minutes or it's more like twenty-two minutes
because of some traffic thing. Or it's a lie that we all base
the truth on: I'll be there in ten minutes. I remember my
Papa telling my Mama he'd be back from the store in ten
minutes. That was twelve years ago. The checkout line
must be wrapped around the Earth—that must be it. Ten

minutes. Ten years. Ten seconds. What does it matter? Why even say anything for that matter? Say "I'll be there when it suits me, you impatient idiot." I would have accepted half an hour if Pip really meant half an hour. But he didn't. He meant: when I get there, idiot. I am at fault, though, as well; I should have said on the phone, "I want you here now" instead of letting him tell me ten minutes. I knew full well I was going to pull my hair out for ten minutes waiting for him to get here, all the while dwelling on the lie perpetuated by every idiot on this Earth of "I'll be there in ten minutes." Ten minutes. Ten idiot minutes. I heard you dream only for a few seconds or minutes even though it could feel like ten minutes or even ten hours. Those are dreams, though; we are allowed to lie and do unnatural things in dreams—look at that! I just called lying unnatural. Christ, that's the most natural thing humans do to themselves, to each other, to pretend gods who live in the sky. Lie lie lie. Ten minutes. Idiot ten minutes—

BEEP BEEP!

He's here. Took him long enough.

I look through the glass that decorates the top of the front door to be sure and run through the rain as he pushes open the passenger door.

"You got money, honey?"

"Maybe."

"Don't play."

"I do. Can we just drive?"

The white four-door Nissan Stanza takes off down Palmetto Street and turns onto Forest Avenue. I don't say a word until we hit the first traffic light.

"Pippy, let me ask you...."

"Here we go."

"Do men get more sad over losing their dog or their lady?"

"Where do you come up with these questions? 'Cause I know you don't really want an answer, you just want me to answer because it's a game to you. You just want to hear an answer."

"I want your answer."

"Like last week when you asked me about the zoo, what was it again—which zoo animal has a better life, the elephants or the polar bears? What kind of stupid shit is that?"

"You told me the elephants because they get to eat hay and poop wherever they want."

"Yeah, that's true. Hahaha, that's very true. But whatta dumb question. I mean, why do you ask this stuff?"

"Why not?"

"You're burnt, Dezzy."

"No, not me. So what about it?"

"What? The dog or the girlfriend thing?"

"Yes. Do men get more sad over losing their dog or their lady?"

"I don't know. I never had any dog. Most women I can take or leave. I don't know. I would probably miss my dog more."

"Why?"

"Dogs are easy, they get to eat hay and shit everywhere, hahahahaha."

What an idiot. I don't think Mr. Jean feels that way, although I am still unsure about what makes him more sad. I need to ask him next time.

The rain is steady and smatters against the windshield through whipping wipers. I think that we could pull over anywhere and do our business. Under the M Train trestle seems right.

"Pull over." Pip is still laughing at his dog answer and quickly turns his head toward me.

"What? That was funny! I said the same answer as the elephant question!"

"Yes, hilarious. Pull over by the trestle there. The rain is hard enough that everyone is inside now. We will be fine. No one can see. Right there. Stop. Shut the engine off."

The car comes to a stop and the downpour drums on the hood of the car. He turns the key and the wipers stop. The sound is beautiful; like closing your eyes and holding your ears closed while in the shower so the rhythmic pitter patter of the drops is all that is left. The rain pulses so hard we can no longer see through the car windows. It is a perfect rain: clear enough that we can make out objects outside, but they are smudged and smeared through the cascading rain flow. Perfect. A prison of sorts. Self-imposed rainstorm prison.

"Let me see the money."

"It's right there in the cup holder." Pip looks down and there sits forty dollars, two rolled twenty-dollar bills.

"Hold out your hand, honey." He drops the white powder baggy into my palm and I squeeze it tight. I squeeze it like I held Papa's hand before he left for the grocery store twelve years ago. I squeeze it like the night I grabbed my bed covers as I was dragged from my bedroom to get a beating in the living room by Mama. I squeeze it like the doll I took on the car ride to Aunt Gloria's house to see my older, evil cousins. I squeeze it until I disappear and I fall asleep right there in Pip's car.

Only I have no dreams.

Everyone is bereft of something at some point and no matter how hard or tight I squeeze my dreams, I can never get them to come back.

I want to know what Mr. Jean missed more. I just have to ask him. Perhaps tomorrow or the day after. At least I will wait until this rain stopped.

It will stop in ten minutes.

a morning with goldie

this is the last time I do this: This is the last straw. No more. No more wine. No more chasing it with scotch. No more thinking it's funny. No more wet stockings. I am not even sure how it happened. You are too old for this, young lady. Sixty-five years old and still eligible for the electric chair. I absolutely do not have the wherewithal to face another night like last. What time is it? Sun is blinding me, it's probably early morning. I know what the morning holds now. I just don't want to face it. And I won't.

I put down the half-wet paper and rub my eyes. I look at it again. The ink is still bleeding down the page, barely readable now, but it still reads the same scripted desperation that comes with the head surfacing from inside of the toilet bowl. Leaving myself a note like this does no good; it's virtually the same as a pep talk the next morning or afternoon about the dangers of continuing to live a life in such a way. Alice noted while in Wonderland that she gave herself such good advice, but she rarely followed it. Ditto, dear Alice. This is Wonderland and I am a wonder gal who thinks to herself, *What a wonderful world*. The wastebasket is overflowing, but I crumple the note up and throw it at the mass of soiled toilet paper, used ear swabs, and other assorted accoutrement that need no details. A lady never tells those tales.

What to do now.

I just have to pray some more. That is the key. Father Morley told me twenty years ago, "Goldie, if you keep drinking like that, if you keep outside late and keep the company of men, and you don't fear the Lord, you are never to reap your heavenly reward. So pray. Pray often: in the morning, pray before supper, pray before slumber. That will keep you in the good graces of God."

He said to think of the beatitudes; the poor shall inherit the Earth and blessed be the sinners or something. A lot of fancy, feel-good, fortuitous stuff. There I was every morning, when I felt really bad from the night before, sort of like now, buying wholesale into all of this blessed be the so-and-so doggerel. After he was satisfied, Father Morley would walk me to the back of the church where two cedar doors would lead to the confession room. There I would confess, but not into detail, all my latest sins. I would tell him mostly everything; what sins I didn't tell him I would pad with made-up, not-so-bad sins. They were always ones that I thought he could handle. Afterwards, he'd ask me to recite Hail Marys until the rhythmic, hypnotizing words transformed into pop song. So I would. The prayers sounded nice and they had some rhythmic sense to them. I find now that I will say them out loud while in the shower or even after seven or so drinks. They still sound nice. Father Morley was always impressed with me and my taking to the prescribed Catholic prayers.

He never did realize I was a Jewish woman.

I have to pee, bad. Bladder is set to spill onto whatever is below it. I will go into the bathroom, but I refuse to look in the mirror. It is dark gray and scratched. I always look alright when I check my hair, my lips, my ass. I never check my teeth. I know how they look by the discomfort I feel. Men don't care about teeth. They don't look for them right away. They pay attention to the tongue and how the words dance off the lips. How, when they talk to you, the tongue will lick the upper lip in approval. They notice that trite horseshit.

Ha. Horseshit is a word that Sam used to use.

Sam. I am sick of seeing him sitting on his stoop talking all kinds of stuff to his neighbors. No one cares. I mean they don't care one bit. He has that whore Puerto Rican girl filing in and out of his apartment like a slave bringing him deli meats and cheeses, sometimes wine and beer, even knitted blankets. Good. Let him have that. Better her fingers than mine. She hands him those homemade sandwiches on bodega-bought bread that she cuts down the middle with a plastic knife that she swiped off the deli counter. I'd stab him *and* her if I could with that goddamn knife. That little Puerto Rican girl or whatever she is shaking her ass with that "Oh Mister Jean, Mister Jean" *mira mira* thing she does. What does he give you, honey? A good spanking while he spanks it into the sink in the bathroom? Why don't you *mira mira* this plastic knife I have in my pocket right here for you? What horseshit!

Christ—I really have to pee.

That can wait. I think. It will have to wait. Come on old girl, time to get up off the bathroom floor, pull it together and head out the front door because the icebox is empty and I could sure use a drink!

Through the windblown spaces between the closed curtains, I notice Keith and Dave shuffling in front of Nunny's Liquors. They are two large, happy dunderheads—but nice large and happy dunderheads. I adore them both.

It's the same old scene: Keith laughing loudly at Dave whispering "dammit, goddammit" repeatedly as he tries to get the keys to fit into the front door padlock. I want to go visit them. I have nothing else to do.

"Boys! Boys, up here! Keith, Dave, up here—you guys opening up?"

Dave doesn't look up at me but hurries through the now-unlocked front door. Keith just waves quickly and disappears into the darkness.

"Keith! I'm coming down! What's today's tasting, honey baby?"

They shut the door without even saying a word! Maybe they couldn't hear me? Keith had waved, waved right at me! Maybe he was waving at someone else waving at him in front of my apartment building or on the street. Maybe it's this goddamn hangover and I imagined him waving when he was just shielding the sun from his eyes. Could I have mistaken that for a wave?

Looking in the mirror now, I am noticing the matted, stringy hair, the deepness of the bags under my eyes, the worry lines on my forehead, and the horrible taste in my mouth and the scent of tooth decay on my breath. I'd punch the mirror if it'd do me any good.

I know those two heard me. They heard me well and good.

Perhaps it wasn't that they hadn't heard me; I've had that feeling in my bones for some time; this disinvited, left-out-of-the-will feeling. Here I am looking in this mirror and I know it to be true. The human incarnation of Willy Loman: they all just eat the fruit and throw away the peel.

Perhaps I am completely wrong—maybe this is spite. I love spite. I can spite from dawn to dusk. And unlike Willy Loman, I will not be huffing on a gas pipe. I need to pee. And I will need a goddamn drink.

I'm going down there. Need my keys, need my shoes, need my handkerchief, my purse—what else? Not looking in the mirror again; I look great. Just need to get out the door.

The rain slows to a drizzle by the time I reach the front door. Street is empty. This neighborhood is always empty mid-morning. Nunny's stands across the street underneath the staircase and holding station of the elevated M train. The green gild provides a perfect shield from the rain, snow, sun—whatever Mother Nature can muster against us. Most days there would be one or two passersby collected underneath, holding their liquor in a brown bag, smoking, sometimes coughing. They never stay long. They never speak to one another except to ask for a light or if the other had a used newspaper they would give away. Sometimes one poor bastard will try and sell the 75-cent *NY Post* for 25. Sometimes the other guy would pay; other times, he'd just turn away and mumble into the brown paper bag. Keith and Dave let it go on as long as no one made too much noise or got hurt. The storefront stands empty today.

I really need to pee.

BANG BANG BANG BANG BANG BANG BANG BANG

Look at this old plastic glass door tremble and vibrate under each of my blows. Good. Let it fall off the hinges. The door has no business being locked anyway—not at this time of day. They should be open now.

BANG BANG

I know they can hear me. I know they are in there listening and giggling to themselves because they know that it's me knocking. I don't care if they pretend they aren't in there so I have to stand here like an old fool. This is spite, that's what it is. Pure spite. And I love spite.

BANG BANG

"I hate spite, you hear in there! You open up, I am not standing here another instant!"

"Stop that banging, Goldie. We'll be open when we're open."

"Dave, goddamn you, open this door."

"We aren't ready for you yet."

"Is Keith inside with you?"

"Hi, sweetheart. We're not ready to open."

"Keith, I'll piss right on the goddamn door."

"Why would you do a thing like that?"

"Didn't you hear me calling out to you idiots?"

"When?"

"Goddamn, you waved after I called to you!"

"I was waving a fly away from my face, sweetheart."

BANG BANG BANG BANG

"Jesus, Goldie, we aren't ready for you yet."

"Oh you're ready for me—just ask Mister Chung here. He is enjoying my banging and yelling while his customers squeeze his grapefruits!"

"Oh he is? Hi, Mister Chung!"

"Hi Keith."

"How are the watermelons this morning?"

"Verr good, Keith."

"Beat it, Chung. Just open the door, Keith. I have to pee. What spirits are we sampling today?"

"Just open the door, Keith," Dave yelled from the back room. "Just let her in already."

I have spent four years inside this liquor store, sampling their products without purchasing a single thing. Keith and Dave have always been nice boys to an old lady like me. I knew them from the neighborhood; they were teenagers hanging around then, usually late afternoons in the school-yards and on street corners where the all-night deli found them at the early part of dawn. They weren't always nice boys then.

I used to live in an old railroad apartment near Sam's Special Mart on Forest and Woodbine Avenues. It was roach-infested in the front of the apartment near the kitchen, bathroom, and part of the living room, but for some reason the swarthy bastards never made their way to the back end of the flat. That's where I parked my ass and slept after a long day of walking and drinking. It had a window that faced the street. The red-and-white fluorescent glow of Sam's Special store sign flooded my room at night and from then on, gentlemen callers referred to my bedroom as the Red Light District Special.

Before sleep, I'd sit on the edge of my bed, the window open, the blinds curled so I could look and listen to the ebb and flow of the avenue. One night, quarter past one, the action began. Keith held court surrounded by a posse of seven or eight guys and always a few giggling half-drunk gals. The boys darted in and out of Sam's buying beers or snacks and talking loudly between some god-awful rock music blaring out of the speakers of what could have been a stolen car. As the beers filled their guts, the temperament of the boys changed, and there would be Keith and Dave in the middle of a scrum by the end of an unintelligible shouting match. Fists and legs flailed as the bodies fell into parked cars and parking meters. The music shut off. Keith separated the two, turned toward Sam's and yelled something toward the shut door where Sam, now hiding behind, was watching. In the distance I could hear the gentle crescendo of police sirens. The end was near. Sam and Keith exchanged words for a moment before Keith turned and threw an empty beer bottle right through the glass window.

CRASH

Behind the blinds I had one hand wrapped around a bottle of Schmidt's beer. The other was dug deep inside my pantie line.

I loved that kind of shit.

That is all over now. Now they own and run Nunny's and are married to women they met on one of those corners. Keith told me one day after a Port wine or two that he got married because he assumed it would be a good idea to be married. Dave doesn't know why he's married. He has two kids. He loves them. I told him I thought he married because of Catholic guilt. It runs rampant in this town. He shrugged his shoulders between sips of port and Bushmill whiskey shooters. I knew that they both loved their ladies though. I envied them between sips of suds and bouts of that Catholic guilt.

I like spending time with them, yelling, listening, over-helping their cash paying customers. They ignore me and my shit for the most part. The boys spend their time unpacking bottles, placing them on shelves, tuning the radio, flirting with the less beat-up gals who wander in the door, befriending the rest, drinking the leftover product, and shrugging their shoulders at most everything.

"My boys! What a beautiful morning!"

Keith shrugs. Dave raises his eyebrows and sighs.

"It's raining, Goldie, and we have a big delivery coming today—Keith, 600 pieces right?"

"Yep."

"Always complaining. It will be just fine."

"No it won't."

"I'll pray for you Dave, don't you worry. What are we drinking today?"

Keith is standing behind the cash register and turns around to face the wall of assorted brown and clear liquors. The bottles stand like patient soldiers, waiting for their time for action. Keith sighs and tilts his head toward me.

"Pick one, sweetheart."

"Just one?"

"It's nine in the morning. How much would you like for me to open?"

"I just would like enough to get us through to lunch."

Keith sighs again and wipes his hands on the dusting rag.

"Open two, ya crazy Jew."

Just as I laugh my bladder shakes and wrings my belly with such a pain.

"Oh, I gotta pee!"

Keith shrugs as he opens the register and fingers the coin slots.

"So, can I use the damn thing?"

"You know where it is, hun."

I hate this damn bathroom. It's built for boys. Small and smelly with no real window to let out the odor of the beer and booze farts those two let out in here all day long. I am not even counting the skylight above that is fitted with a fan; it doesn't draw out the air, but it does spin and sound like a turbine engine warming up at old Idlewild Airport. Ahh, Idlewild. Never will call it John F. Kennedy airport, not me—I didn't vote for him. I didn't vote for anyone, actually. I can never find the light, either. Screw it. I'll just sit in the dark. Might be a good time to send one of those Father Morley prayers up to heaven before this day starts. Best to keep my head low; anything to avoid anymore of this rotted onion and bile smell. Let us pray:

> Mother Mary, pray for us
> Jesus, Son of God, pray for us
> Holy Spirit or Ghost, pray for us
> Owner of 12 Sons Deli on Forest Avenue, pray
> for me

Prayers done. Piss done. Panties back up. It's pudding time.

As I exit the bathroom I hear the two boys laughing and listening to music while they stock the shelves.

"I prayed for you in the bathroom, Dave."

Keith laughs. Dave doesn't.

"Please don't think of me when you're in the bathroom."

"Did you pour me a sample?"

Keith turns around and produces three small plastic cups filled with silver champagne. He hands me one still foaming at the top. It fizzes and licks the tip of my nose as I bring it to my lips.

"A little bubbles for me and little bubbles for you and—how about you, Dave?"

"Nah, I'm okay—maybe once this order is unloaded."

"More for me!" I shout. Keith laughs. Dave shrugs.

"Cheers." Keith flashes a large smile and taps the cup against mine.

The front door is fastened with two garden bells that chime every time it swings open or closed. It is this that causes our Pavlov reaction to jerk our heads and look up.

CHING CHING.

"Hi fellas, hi Miss Goldie." The scratching on the green-and-white tiled floor belongs to the paws of Jim Douglas's Spitz pup, Tabitha. She heads straight behind the counter where Keith is waiting for her with a milk bone. Jim heads right for the fishbowl on the counter full of Absolut vodka nips. He fingers the bottles and pulls one out and stuffs it in his front pocket. He immediately starts speaking. "So, there I was, walking the Tabitha, ya know, right down Woodbine

Street, right near the Church, and I sees these two stupid bananas fighting in the street. It was a young boy and young girl, I dunno. They were fist fighting."

I sip my drink and watch Jim as he takes another vodka nip and shoves it in his other jacket pocket. Keith is nodding and listening as he nuzzles his face in Tabitha's yellow and brown, full-grown fur. Her winter coat is thick enough to nod me off to slumber. Dumb dog. Dumb Keith. He doesn't even realize Jim is swiping the nips.

"So the dog starts getting scared and I yells at them, 'Hey Ho Hey, cut that shit out!' And they stop for a minute and look up. So naturally Tabitha don't care, now she wants to do her business, so she starts peeing on the car right near where they were fighting."

"You did, Tabitha? Good dog, good dog!" Keith gives her another milk bone and nuzzles his face again.

"So I think it's over, right? And I turn to light up a smoke and sip a nip and then the two bananas start yelling and fighting again! I says to myself, it's seven thirty in the morning and these two are gonna have the cops here any minute so I yank on Tabitha's leash, like this, and speed walk off."

Dave calls from across the room. "I bet the cops came two minutes later!"

"And the cops came not two minutes later! So I was only half a block away because Tabitha kept pulling the leash toward the trees, you know how she gets and, she's been wetting the floor now and again so I says to myself let her do her business out here."

"Yeah, you gotta let her." Keith looks sad as he stares at Tabitha now.

Jim looks down at her wagging tail. "She's no spring chicken."

I smooth my arm across Jim's jacket right near the stolen nips. "Neither am I, baby."

"Yeah, Goldie, well, you know it's not just the dog, my legs, too. They aren't right anymore really. I can't walk the way I used to, but it worked out because I got to see the cops come and throw the two of them bananas in the back of the car." Jim pulls another nip out of the fishbowl, opens it, drains it, and produces a dollar and five cents from his back jean pocket. "This should cover it, Keith."

"Sure, just leave it on the counter. You want a little bubbles?"

"Nah, none for me, I gotta get her outta here. I don't want her peeing on your floor."

"I almost peed on the floor before, Jim." The boys ignore my sarcasm.

"I'll see ya later. Keep the doors locked; the crazies are running around town today."

"We always do. I always have the Beretta next to the register."

Jim pushes the door open and lets Tabitha go first. After the door closes, I notice a slight wet trail on the floor leading to the door.

CHING CHING

"Ya know Goldie, I love that damn dog more than my wife."

Dave laughs from across the room.

"What do you mean? That dog is peeing all over the place."

"She's still better than my wife." Keith turns to Dave as he giggles. "Yep, better than mine too."

"Well Mister Keith, while you had your face buried in that dog's ass Jim was lifting nips."

"I know that."

"Oh."

"It's Jim who is incontinent, you know."

CHING CHING

I never have a chance to ask how he knew that because our heads all turn to the door.

In walks Tina. She is in her usual uniform: faded stone-washed jeans and an oversized grey sweatshirt with the sleeves cut off. Her Native American necklace bought roadside at her cousin's government-issued reserve has been attached to her since she was a teenager. She is good and drunk with a fresh vodka smile and constantly runs her hands through her 1985 haircut. I like her. She likes girls. I still like her. She, like Jim, speaks right away. "Oh, well hey, what's going on in here, guys?"

"Just tasting some bubbles. Here is one for you," Keith hands her Dave's cup.

"Oh, I like that. Goldie hun, shouldn't you be at church?"

"We *are* at church, sweetheart."

Keith makes the sign of the cross over us. "Bless you. Bless you, one and all."

We drink the silver suds in one shot.

"Much needed Keith, thanks," says Tina.

I wrap my arm around her waist and whisper in her ear. "I already prayed in the toilet."

Tina laughs and runs her fingers through her hair. Keith is busy tuning the radio and refilling our cups, and I hadn't noticed Dave is pacing around the store, one end to the other, in a rhythmic march. He keeps checking the windows, his watch, his wallet, his phone, his pockets—I guess for the delivery truck. I wonder why he doesn't shrug about that, like he does everything else. It's just a delivery. We have booze, music, and time for our own. I didn't feel so bad anymore. I hadn't looked in the mirror either. I take a sip of the champagne and point towards Tina. "So, where you coming from, Ms. Tina?"

"From the beach. Rockaway. Beach 121. Went real early with my neighbor Earl. You know him, Keith; he comes in here and buys cases of the Grand Macnish Scotch."

"Ahh, yes I do."

"Yes you do. Well, we went early and I love going with him because he has all the great sinkers and lures, ya know? Plus he brings that scotch with him and we sip and cast before anyone else gets there. It's real nice. Oh, and he also knows all the cops since his brother Fred, God rest his soul, was a famous sergeant or something in the seventies. So they never bother us. We just fish and sip until we don't want to fish and sip anymore."

She drains her champagne and Keith walks over to the fridge. He slides the door back and produces the bottle to refill her cup.

"You catch much?"

Tina takes a sip and points to the blue cooler she walked in with. "Yep, four stripers. Rest was seaweed."

"Earl must have caught too, right? He's a beast out there."

"He did a little, but asked mostly about you, Goldie."

I don't care. "Why me? He had you to go fish with already. Bastard never comes around anymore."

Keith laughs. "You tossed his fishing poles off the Rockaway Bridge last summer."

Keith is right. "It was tequila's fault," I say in defeat.

Tina grabs my arm. "He said he wished he could use you as bait."

"Oh please. That was the scotch talking. Earl is a drinker and a fisherman; he don't have it in him to hurt anyone."

Tina drinks the rest of her cup. "I dunno."

"Well, it sounds like you guys have a good time there." Keith bends over the cooler and opens the lid examining the fish inside. They are beautiful bass, all eight to nine pounders with a striking white and gold mix across their slick bodies.

"We did, and we do. But today was different."

Keith tops off our cups. "How so?"

Just then the door opens as Tina answers.

CHING CHING

"Earl told me he murdered his cousin last night."

Pavlov response and everyone turns. The slow shuffle of feet and tap of a borrowed cane means bad news. It is the spy of all spies. Despite him carrying a plate full of homemade Italian cookies, old Mario always reeks of rotten, bad news. He comes in for one thing: to listen and rat us all out.

The air in Nunny's grows quiet.

He waves his cane and mumbles something. Keith knows how to handle it.

"Hi Mario, have a seat over here. What ya got there? Looks like cookies?"

He nods and mumbles.

"Thank you. They look great. Did you make them this morning?"

He nods and mumbles as he sits down.

"Oh good, and look at that, you dripped honey and sprinkles on them."

Mario shrugs and waves his cane. I hate this guy.

"Well, I'll put them out and let everyone have a taste. Customers will love it. Did you want a sample of the champagne we are selling today?"

He shrugs his shoulders and taps his cane a few times on the floor.

Keith hands him a cup and no one says a word. Mario sniffs the drink and brings it to his lips. It grows even quieter. What if he heard Tina say Earl murdered his cousin? Who would he tell? What could he actually do and how far would any of this go? I hate Mario. Spineless old waste of life. Before he drinks he looks at me hard. I stare back. He looks at Tina. Tina runs her fingers through her hair. Dave paces. Keith eats a cookie. Somewhere a baby is born.

Mario drinks the cup down and sets it on a box of wine displayed next to him. He stands up. No one speaks. As he flashes his remaining teeth, he begins loudly tapping his cane on the floor and pointing in our direction. I begin to feel bad again: tired, old, worn. I don't want to be here.

Mario turns to Keith and waves his cane again; his feet shuffle out the door.

"Okay, Mario, thanks again for the cookies. Get home safe." Through more mumbling he tilts his head back enough to hear us mutter as much as a whisper. Then he disappears through the front door.

CHING CHING

Tina fits her earphones on and thanks Keith for the drink. Then she, too, is gone.

CHING CHING

"More for you, I guess?" asks Keith. I look at Dave. He has stopped pacing. The delivery truck rolls up in front of the store.

PART 4

they call him Corporal benjamin Zogby

orraine sat quietly on the bottom step of her gray-painted stoop. She surveyed the length of Cypress Avenue, taking in the telephone poles and the long, black, sleek wires that were suspended high above the avenue like a circus tightrope. The poles and wire cables lined every street for miles and miles; Lorraine imagined herself being shrunk down to the size of a squirrel and running along those wires, passing over stoops that looked just like her own. She sometimes dreamed that she could run on those wires far away from Cypress Avenue, but she also knew they would just lead her to another avenue, just like this one, with a misnomer for a name. Such avenues like Forest, Grandview, Fairview, St. Nicholas avenues; none of which boasted a grand or fair view or bore any resemblance to a forest and certainly did not house any saints. There was also Onderdonk Avenue but what the hell was an Onderdonk?

Lorraine sighed. Then sat quietly again, this time listening. In the apartment building next door, her neighbors were yelling at one another; about what she wasn't quite sure, but it was louder than usual. They had left the front windows of the first-floor railroad apartment open this time. They were a not-so-young couple who took to yelling at one another almost every day since as far back as Lorraine could remember. What they argued about never made sense; they just didn't seem to like each other much. Usually the arguing was just some muffled ambient noise that mixed in with the half-chirping birds and rolling engines of passing cars and buses. The usual sounds of Cypress Avenue.

An old car, slow-moving, rolled by and Lorraine turned her eyes to where the wheels had once been. Cypress Avenue had unremarkable streets; they were dotted with rusting sewer caps and flanked by aging sewer grates. Cigarette butts lined the gutters like confetti while gum tar and pressed bottle caps splashed across the length of the avenue. It could have been a Jackson Pollock painting. Lorraine looked to the sidewalks to see if they meant something different. They didn't. The sidewalks led to stoops that led to linoleum-lined stairs that led to six floor-walks ups. Lorraine was sick of six floor-walks ups. She was sick of six floor-walks downs. The apartments were hot and full of bugs and they were everywhere.

She wanted out.

Maybe, it would be okay to visit now and again. She liked the train tracks and the trolley rails that would sometimes peek out from the worn-out, paved-over cobblestone roads. The schoolyards with their silver-painted fencing that sometimes had swing sets sitting behind them that she could swoosh back and forth on through the Ridgewood air; high enough to almost touch those phone pole wires. The bodegas and laundromats her mother frequented lined the corners of every few blocks; and the corners after that were topped with bus stops where buses barely showed up. The opened and now-milked Johnny pumps were in between those corners. Lorraine hated corners. She had been hanging around them long enough. Corners and mechanic chop shops and Irish bars and Polish bars and bars that didn't identify with any one heritage at all—just sloppy joints full of sloppy people. The entire neighborhood that Cypress Avenue filled seemed to be a facsimile; all gray and on repeat from one end to the other. Lorraine had enough now. She wanted out, and this time, she meant it this time more than the last.

SLAM!

The neighbor's window crashed shut. The yelling continued but back to its usual muffle. The funny thing was, the birds had never stopped chirping. It all seemed so normal.

Just then, frantic footsteps raced towards Lorraine's stoop. She looked up. It was Lolly; her hair waved wildly around her face while she smiled and laughed through huge intakes of air. She grabbed Lorraine's hand and yanked her up.

"RUN! He's after me!"

Startled, Lorraine got up and took off with Lolly, giggling and yelling right behind her. The two girls both ran across the sidewalks that Lorraine hated and jumped over the gutters that Lorraine hated and drifted across the streets that Lorraine hated in a wild marathon sprint down the length of Cypress Avenue. Behind them, angry yells from old man Fu echoed off the cramped-together railroad apartment buildings until they made enough space between their steps and his yells. The racket gradually faded away into the bird chirping, neighbor yelling, and car rumbling of the avenue.

The girls stopped running and immediately plopped down against the brown Mr. T dumpster that was chained and locked to the storefront of 12 Sons Deli. It had to be chained and locked there because every few weeks someone would show up and try and steal it. No one knew who or why someone would steal a dumpster, but it was always found later the following day only a few blocks away. Ralph, the owner of 12 Sons Deli, would look over the metal barge, grunt a little, wheel it back to the storefront, and place it back where it belonged without a word. Now it was locked up. No one had tried to steal it since. It all seemed so normal.

Both girls were catching their breath now, Lolly still laughing through what sounded like a smoker's cough. A pair of elderly women shuffling along the sidewalk didn't look their way but scoffed as they walked by; Lolly just stuck her tongue out at them. They kept going. No one ever stopped. It was best to keep walking until you got off this avenue.

Lorraine collected herself and slowly looked up to the green-painted street signs to see exactly where they were: it was the corner of Cypress Avenue and Woodbine. *Another goddamn corner*, Lorraine thought to herself. A bird landed on the phone wires above and chirped. Lorraine sighed. It was time to find out why Lolly was running away from old man Fu. When she finally asked, Lolly belted a few coughs and half-laughs, then shook her head no.

"It's a long story and it isn't really that funny."

Lorraine nodded. She was probably right. There was *no need* to talk about what just happened. None of it was very funny anymore. It all used to be funny, but that was when Lolly and Lorraine had first met. That was now almost three years ago. Everything had become so changeless. Here they were again: playing hooky from summer school, standing on another corner laughing at some stupid nonsense. Lorraine was tired of the usual neighborhood banter. It was all the same changeless gray. She stood up and turned to Lolly with something new.

"Guess what?"

Lolly stared at her.

"No man is innocent. I am going to get that tattooed on my right shoulder in black ink."

Lolly coughed. "Why?"

"I dunno. My uncle says that a lot."

"Which uncle? Your dad's or your mom's brother?"

"My dad's brother would never be clever enough to say something like that aloud, even if he could dream up such a thing—I don't care how many PhDs he has."

"How many does he have?"

Lorraine sighed. "Just one. But it doesn't matter. It's my mom's brother who said it anyway."

"Oh. He's kind of old, right?"

"Yeah. Well, not that old."

"I saw your uncle sitting on his stoop a few times. I was walking home from school and he was out there just staring. I think it was him."

"Did he have a Styrofoam cup and a cap on?"

"I think so."

"Well, that was him."

"Aww, he's old and cute."

Lorraine stared at the green-painted street signs.

"I wonder what he meant...."

"About what?"

"About all men not being innocent."

"Wasn't he in the Army?"

"I think the Marines."

"Well, maybe he was talking about that."

"About the Army?"

Lolly coughed and laughed again. "No about men and war and shit like that."

"I dunno what he meant. I just really like the way it sounds. No man is innocent."

"Me too."

"Actually, no one is innocent."

Lolly pointed at Lorraine. "Except you, you virgin!"

"You're a virgin, too!"

"Not for long. But, well, maybe...you're right, we are all innocent."

Lorraine didn't understand the remark. "How do you figure that?"

Lolly leaned against the dumpster and fiddled with the lock before she spoke. "It's because we really only live life once and everything that happens is for the first time, right?

You can't be born more than once or die more than once or even walk down the same street the same way more than once. So everything is one take, no do-overs. Therefore, we are innocent."

"Hahahaha. Where is this coming from?"

"I dunno, I was just thinking about it and it came out. We are all innocent. First time offenders for life."

"You are just trying to let yourself off the hook for whatever it is you're feeling guilty about."

"We all make excuses. And in that excuse we can be innocent."

"Well, according to my uncle, not men."

"I wonder why?"

Lorraine walked over and leaned on the dumpster now too, her face close to Lolly's. "Hey, let's go ask him."

"Yeah, you should ask him what the hell it means before you tattoo it on your arm. Hey, maybe he will give us beer."

"Definitely, I drank a few with him last Thanksgiving. He lives just like fifteen blocks from here, let's walk the tracks, it's quicker. One thing though, he will want us to call him Corporal, not uncle, okay?"

"Why?"

"I dunno—even my mother calls him Corporal now. His name is Benjamin. But he doesn't like anything but Corporal."

"Should I salute him too?"

"Just be nice."

They made their way to the opening in a metal fence that encompassed the freight train tracks. The wooden boards were brown and warm, the rails not so much. Lolly and

Lorraine always stayed off them despite there being no electricity running through the American-bred steel. Lorraine liked to kick the placed gravel about as she walked and talked, paying close attention to the sounds reaching out from the distance. Most time it was a train, or even a patrol car, that somehow got down to the freight line tracks to foxhound transients. The pair never knew exactly where the rails ultimately led to. Sometime they'd stay off them, then run through the blades of unmanicured grass and wild brush into the ever-present expanse of suburb and city yelling to each other that they had to just make it out and get away. When the danger was quite far behind them, they'd step into the sunlight and sit in an aborigine park full of worn picnic tables. They were once painted red, but now they sit winter-chipped and devoid of dinner. The tables stood, a lone testament to the first kisses of coming-of-age girls and boys, right off the main drag of their parent's fairway in the final cut of summertime.

Today the tracks lead to Lorraine's Uncle Benjamin's apartment. The girls held hands as a wind kicked up a little and whooshed through the tops of the tree leaves. The birds went silent.

&

Zogby rubbed his hand across his chin. He was watching the ash on the end of the cigarette grow. It was quite long now. Below the hand that held the cigarette was his foam white cup full of Schmidt's beer. He didn't move his hand for fear the ash would fall into the suds and so the ash could make its way to the concrete below. Zogby just waited and watched. Something would have to give soon enough.

An engine roar and squeak of air brake sounded just across the street. Zogby didn't move his head but tipped his eyes upward, away from the ash gaze, to watch the big wheels come to rest in front of the bus stop. No one got off, no one got on. The bus waited a moment, its doors open and its engines off. Perhaps it waited for Zogby. He thought of that for a moment before rubbing his chin and turning his eyes back to his ash and beer. The engine turned back on, the doors closed, and the wheels turned back to the road.

Out of the corner of his eye a woman darted out of the corner store and ran down the street shouting at the bus, "Wait! Wait!" Her black shoes kicked through the puddles and pus of Ridgewood's streets, her arms outstretched. She knew as much as anyone else the next bus would be an hour or so away during midday. She had to make this bus.

Dust and exhaust kicked up right into her outstretched arms, but she ran even faster, screaming after the bus, "Wait! Wait! No!" Zogby watched as her feet fell underneath one another and her chest slammed down into the ground, skidding her body across the wet walkway. She lay motionless.

When she finally moved again, she screamed and cursed into the fresh exhaust; her mouth now pressed against the sidewalk inadvertently lapping up rain water. She lay there for a moment before picking herself up and looked at Zogby. Her finger pointed straight at him and its end dripped with puddle water.

"You saw me coming! You could have stopped the bus, right? You saw me!"

Zogby looked back down to the ash. It hadn't fallen off his cigarette yet. That was luck. His eyes turned back up to the woman. She was crying and staring at her hands now. She checked her watch and punched her leg. There was nothing she could do but walk in the direction of the bus.

Zogby took the white Styrofoam cup and brought it to his mouth. He swallowed. Then he looked at his cigarette. The ash was gone. Zogby looked into his drink, rubbed his chin. *It all goes to the same place*, he thought.

The apartment building Zogby lived in faced the street, and across from there it faced another identical apartment building. He never noticed anyone coming or going from that side of Cypress Avenue. He had lived in the same building for the last forty-five years; raised his family on the food the side-street market stands offered, had picnics in the Cypress cemetery which always doubled as a park for working stiffs with little pocket money, and had his two children blessed and baptized at St. Aloysius Church. He and his family were mutts living among the German and Irish who imbedded in the area during the roaring twenties.

Zogby adjusted the brim of his cap and smoothed his fingers across the stitched yellow thread that carried across the top. It wasn't in braille, although at times he thought it might be. No one noticed the large letters that spelled out U.S. ARMY VETERAN and underneath KOREA 68–71 blazed with eagles holding the American flag in their beaks. He rubbed his hands down to the back of his neck and reached down for the Styrofoam cup again.

"No one gives a steaming crap," he muttered into the white mouth of the cup.

He opened his eyes and noticed an image reflecting in the gold liquid. It wasn't his. It was Betty's. She was smiling, her lips painted bright red and parted just enough to show light stains on young teeth. Her brown curls fell across her shoulders and onto her breast, curls Zogby used to run his fingers through to try and straighten out. Betty would just laugh at him. "You can't straighten these curls out, ya bum!" But it did not matter; he tried anyway. Her hair was long and full but it did not cover the silver necklace that carried a heart pendant Zogby gave her on their third and final date. He asked for her hand in marriage the next morning. Betty agreed. Her father did not. Zogby and Betty signed the license at City Hall the next day. She was seventeen, he was nineteen. The following week he shipped out to some foreign land where he did not speak the language or understand the ramifications of warfare. Betty sent him letters. He sent some back. She read the ones her father didn't intercept and throw in the incinerator. He sent her a picture of him with some of the boys from his unit. Betty hid that picture under her pillow during the night and the mattress during the day. At least that's what she told him when he returned almost two years later. 1952.

The door of his apartment building opened behind him, startling him out of his daydream. He reached into his shirt's right front pocket and felt inside. The photograph was still there. He pressed it hard against his chest and slowly turned around. It was Father John White.

"That cigarette has gone out Corporal, want another?"

Zogby looked down at his fingers and found just a filter between them. He frowned before he answered. "I only smoke Kents. You smoke that hippy Indian crap."

Father White laughed. "Well...I shouldn't smoke anything, but if I do, I reckon it's that hippy Native-American tobacco, yes. Fine mornin', aint it?"

Zogby turned his head away and reached for his lighter. He flicked it on and let it go out.

"I was a-watchin' from my window and saw that poor young lady take a fall runnin' for that bus. Such a shame. Bus driver has no manners t'all."

Zogby turned back to Father White, who was now standing with his hands on his hips. He was wearing a white Sunday suit with a pocket watch and chain in his coat pocket. His thick cologne was of the Old Spice variety. It masked the cigarettes and scotch. Zogby rubbed his chin. "Preacher, you moved to New York from Alabama about twenty-five years ago. How is it you still speak with that Southern slang? You should be speaking Spanish by now, living in this neighborhood."

"Aw, well, some things you just can't get rid of. It's in my bones now, well, like breathing. I don't even think about it."

"You should start thinking about it." Zogby muttered into his cup again. A sense of irritation came over his body; he never liked Father John White. He was a full-of-shit preacher always looking for a handout that was not for the poor but for himself. The world wouldn't miss a man like that, no matter if he was of the proverbial cloth or of the blue-collar kind. Zogby instinctively reached for his left shirt pocket and felt the compact shape hidden beneath the blue plaid. He always had it there. There was a photograph in his right pocket and this in the other. They both had uses and he thought about them often, sometimes at the same time. Father White had his face up to the sky smiling. Zogby moved his hand away from his left pocket and thought he better not.

"Yep, me and the South still have a love affair. I reckon I'll be buried next to my pappy when I die."

"Your pappy."

"That's right. My ma, now, she is still alive, God bless her." Father White made the sign of the cross and kissed his hand before he raised it to the sky. "And she and my pappy, well, they ain't never got along. Oh boy, she and him would fight and fight through the summers and the winters. She told me, 'John, when I die, I ain't never gonna be buried next to your pappy, 'cause even in the grave we'd just disagree!'"

"Your pappy."

"Yes, she and my pappy."

Zogby lit up another cigarette and blew the smoke into the air. He wished Father White would go to the church or heal the sick or whatever it was he did during the day. At night Zogby knew what he was up to. That was the real Father White. This version was watered down and filtered through the lens of expectation and dollar signs.

"I am on my way to the church, Corporal. Why don't you come today? Do you some good." Father White laid his hand on Zogby's shoulder. "We could light a candle for Betty."

Zogby sucked on the cigarette deep and followed it up with a swig from the Styrofoam cup. He blew out a huge cloud of smoke and coughed. "No." Betty wasn't dead, but she might as well be. At least that's what he told everybody.

"Well, I'll say a prayer for her today...and you too, Corporal. God bless you. I'll see you later on." Father White tugged on his jacket and walked down the stoop steps onto the wet sidewalk. The overpowering scent of Old Spice hit Zogby's nose. He didn't flinch. He never did.

Father White disappeared down the length of Cypress Avenue and into the thickening morning fog, his white suit still visible along with the red brake lights of cars waiting for the traffic light to turn green. It grew quiet.

Zogby flicked the lighter on and watched the flame sway and move ever so slightly. He let it go out and put it back in his right shirt pocket. It lay right next to the photograph now.

"Betty," he whispered to himself.

The fog slowly moved down Cypress Avenue, filling the air in front of his apartment building. The street was empty now. No cars. No buses. No falling ladies. No preachers. No one to give a flying steaming crap about anything.

"My Betty." Zogby rubbed his chin as he set down the Styrofoam cup. He reached into the pocket now and touched the photograph. It was smooth and glossy under his fingers. It felt good. He quickly pulled it out and brought it close to his eyes.

It was a worn black-and-white photo of him and Betty standing together on a beach next to an old clam shack. Written in black ink across the white bottom part of the photo it read, "To my most favorite Betty and Ben in the world, may that world be your oyster! I mean clam!" Zogby smiled and looked up into the fog. The scent of Old Spice had morphed into saltwater air, the stoop into sea-worn boardwalk covered in hot tan sand, the dark of Cypress Avenue into sunlit Cross Bay Boulevard. Zogby himself felt lighter, fit, and free. He heard Betty's big laugh. A warmth came over him as he felt the ghost grip of her small hand in his. She was a fragile woman in body, no more than five feet tall and full of soft features. Her cheeks were dotted by two dimples, her brown eyes surrounded by nearly-visible freckles; eyelashes were thick and batted constantly between moments of conversation. Zogby's mind flooded with images. The beach was full again: there was Sunny's clam shack and Dominic's hot dog truck alongside the boulevard. Next to them was Kenneth Wayne's Bait and Tackle shop, where you could grab a soda and a bucket of snails for two dollars. Full-figured men and women lay on beach towels under umbrellas, munching on freshly barbecued hamburgers and bay shrimp. There were children everywhere; some diving off the pier, others digging for clams in the sand, both stalked by seagulls and hungry hermit crabs. Betty loved the beach. She loved it all. Maybe she loved too much.

"Betty," Zogby mouthed her name but not a whisper came out.

The day was full of clam-slurping and ocean-swimming. Betty fancied herself a fisherman, so they spent a good two hours perched on the pier with poles and lines deep into the bay hoping to hook a good eating fish or two. She would cast spells into the sea air to send the fish their way. It never worked. Betty never gave in. "It will work, ya bum, you wait and see!"

"Ya bum," Zogby whispered.

No fish came and they didn't care. They were married for five years at that time.

A deep male voice entered the air. It hovered over the clam shack and the sand like a cloud crossing the sun. "My most favorite Betty and Ben in the world!" No face. Just a voice. Zogby looked around. Betty was gone. The air grew colder. A plane roared overhead.

SCREEEEEECH SHHHHHHHH

Zogby was startled to see a large blue bus stopped in front of his stoop. The doors opened. A young boy exited through the back door and hopped on his skateboard. The doors closed and the bus pulled away into the now-dissipating fog. Zogby rubbed his chin again and whispered: "Betty."

"Uncle?"

Zogby looked up. It was his niece Lorraine. He didn't answer her.

"I mean, Corporal?"

Zogby reached down for his Styrofoam cup and put the cigarette to his mouth. He pulled on it. Nothing. He thought perhaps the cigarette went out. All that was left was a filter.

"Dammit," he muttered.

"Are you okay, uh…Corporal?"

Zogby reached around for his cigarettes. "Shouldn't you be in school?"

Lorraine looked at Lolly. Lolly took over.

"No sir, Corporal sir, we have Veterans Day off today."

Lorraine hit Lolly in the arm. They both giggled. Zogby did not giggle.

"Today isn't Veterans Day. Don't you see that I am wearing a veteran's hat?"

Lolly shrugged. "So? I mean, sir?"

"So don't you think I might know when Veterans Day is?"

Lorraine pushed Lolly aside and took over. "We played hooky today. We want to get tattoos."

Lolly laughed and jumped in front of Lorraine. "No, your *niece* wants to get a *tattoo*, not *me*. And it's a *tattoo* of something you said, sir!"

Zogby grunted and sipped on the suds. They didn't do much to hush up children. Just to quiet the mind for a short time.

"What's that?" Lorraine was pointing at the photograph. Zogby, forgetting the photo was still out, panicked and shoved it back in his front pocket without answering.

"Ooo, an old picture! Lorraine! I love old pictures! Can we see it, Corporal Uncle sir?"

Zogby stared at Lolly. He rubbed his chin and reached back into his shirt's right pocket, produced the lighter and lit it right in Lolly's face. She jumped back and screamed a little. Lorraine giggled. Zogby let the flame die and put the lighter away. He turned his head and noticed that Lorraine had sat on the stoop right next to him.

"Can I have a beer, Corporal?"

"How old are you, seven?"

"No, fifteen."

"And how old are you?"

Lolly saluted him. "I am twenty-one, sir!"

Zogby reached around his back and threw a beer at Lolly. Lorraine stood up and yelled in protest.

"Hey! She's not twenty-one!"

Lolly cracked the top and took a sip, laughing.

"You're not twenty-one! I'm serious, she is not twenty-one!"

Zogby shrugged and turned to his niece. "She said she was."

"Well, so am I!"

"You said you were fifteen."

"I'm twenty-one."

"We don't lie on Veterans Day, my dear."

Lolly laughed and drank the beer. Her face changed a little as the suds hit the back of her tongue. The beer was warm and it tasted old. She gagged a little. Zogby looked at her and reached back for his lighter. Lolly put the beer down. She felt sick and annoyed now.

"Lorraine, tell him about the tattoo."

"Yes, Lorraine, tell me all about it." Zogby fumbled for another cigarette.

"I dunno, I think I am just gonna go home," Lorraine turned to Lolly, who was now trying to spit any taste of the beer from her mouth into the street.

"No, darling, let me know before you go. I'll get you a beer."

Lorraine looked back at Lolly. She was bent over and mumbling. "No thanks," Lorraine decided.

Zogby shrugged. Lorraine looked at her watch and decided to get on with it. "Well, it was something Momma told me you said once."

"Your momma? I said a lot of stuff to your momma."

"She said you told her a long time ago."

"Everything is a long time ago. Hell, your friend the drunk over there is an old twenty-one." Lolly was still spitting in the street.

"Momma told me you told her after Aunt Betty disappeared." A plane roared overhead, its engine muffling Lorraine's voice.

Zogby pointed to his ears. "Speak up! Those damn planes."

Lorraine sighed. She was frustrated with the whole thing. She didn't care when he said it or why he said it. She cared only that it had some meaning before she inked the words into the fleshy part of her shoulder. The sound of the plane faded into the distance. "Okay! Did you say to Momma that no man is innocent?"

The words caused Zogby's hand to shudder. The cigarette fell, rolled off the stoop, and sank into the wet sidewalk. An ugly pain came over his stomach, like a fish hook through the cheek. The once-scent of ocean brine turned into a smoldering soot. He couldn't stop it. Betty. The deep voice from his daydream drifted again into his head. The best Betty in the world. The best Ben. The best Ben in the world. The best *beds* of other men. *Other* men. Zogby's trembling hand reached for the Styrofoam cup and brought it to his now-dry lips for relief, but it began to crush as his fingers clenched. The beach scene was gone. Zogby remembered it all now.

"Uncle?"

"Call me Corporal."

"Did you say that to Momma?"

He eyes remained fixated on the suds. "That's right I did."

Lolly backed away a bit. "Lorraine, is he okay?"

A sense of cold filled the air and the two girls looked around them: the fog seemed to be rolling back down the avenue.

Zogby looked up at Lorraine and rubbed his chin. He noticed how much she reminded him of Betty; small, fragile, mostly sweet, full of life. He rubbed his front left shirt pocket. It was still there, hard, cold, waiting. He felt his right pocket. She was still there, too. Betty. How he missed Betty. Lorraine looked around as the fog squeezed the avenue tightly. He motioned for Lorraine to come closer to him. As the fog grew thicker, Zogby reached into his front left pocket. Then he spoke.

"I hoped you would be here when the truth came out."

"What truth, Uncle?"

"The best truth one can be taught before they graduate high school."

"I don't understand."

"You will."

Lolly tugged on Lorraine's arm. "Lorraine, let's just get out of here." Lolly turned and kicked the beer over that Zogby gave her.

Lorraine looked back at her uncle. "Will I know why no man is innocent?"

"You already know."

"But I am scared that I know."

"I am too."

A scream and a gun shot rang at the same time the bus rushed across Cypress Avenue. The bus passed the stop. No one got off. Maybe the woman that fell would finally get on up ahead. That's a hefty maybe. No one really gave a flying steaming crap anyway. It was good now. The truth came out. The street was empty again.

PART 5

SONS

The postman let the handle of his carriage go and hurried up the long, grey-painted steps of the stoop carrying a small parcel and a stack of letters. His Buster Brown's faux leather work shoes tapped each step loudly as he went. There were nineteen in all and he counted them in his head every morning. Today he was out of breath and took to counting them through puffs and whispers. *Fifteen, sixteen, seventeen, eighteen, nineteen.* The top step was slippery and he slid a little. There was a faint hope in him that the little slide would turn into a full-blown slip and then into a back injury so he could workers comp his way out of this whole thing. The hope never manifested, however; not when he wanted it to.

He put the letters in his mouth and used the free hand to push the glass hallway door open. He paused. The faint ring of church bells sounded in the distance. *St. Aloysius,* he thought. A simple musical version of a hymn preceded a rhythmic count to sound the day's hour. It was a familiar sound, but today it felt strange as the tones hung on the fog that had settled over Ridgewood proper. It was the church bells' hourly chime that usually helped chip away the day.

As each hour would pass and those satisfying bells had rung, the sun would slide across the sky and cast deeper and longer shadows over his route.

The postman wore a watch; his son had given it to him on their last Father's Day together. Father and son took pictures and threw a football around. After they had dinner, they even smoked a cigar and sipped scotch in the backyard. The postman was proud of his son and his new watch. The watch had stopped working a month after that. He frowned. No matter.

The postman counted the belling while picking and sorting the pieces of mail so he could distribute them to the appropriate slots. As he filled each slot up, he took notice of some of the writing on the front of each one: Con Edison electric and heat, an issue of *The Pennysaver*, mortgage lenders, dental appointment reminders, a very stuffed envelope that read open immediately in red across the front, The Family of Samuel Jean....

"Oh, this goes across the street," he said to no one in particular. Twelve Friends of John O'Malley for City Council flyers, ten new recycling rules pamphlets, and seventeen Chinese menus. There were only six families in the building.

The church bells had stopped. "Dammit," muttered the postman. He lost count reading the Happy Dragon Garden's menu. "Goddamn dammit. Well, it must be ten or so by now."

Time mattered today. He wanted to finish his route by noon. It was a long drive to Sing Sing correctional, and he hadn't seen his son in several months. There was no more putting the visit off. Instinctively, the postman checked the broken watch on his wrist. It still read the wrong time. *Son of a bitch*, he thought. *I have to be done by noon. The Taconic will be bumper-to-bumper by 3:00 p.m. Dammit. There is nothing worse than sitting in traffic on that narrow shit road with the state of radio in New York. They offer absolutely nothing to listen to and they leave it on repeat. In its place what do I get? Brake squeaks. For scenery? The same five trees and a sea of red taillights. Finally it will be the bevy of constipated people driving at the wheel meters away from me that I get to keep me company. I gotta drive to goddamn Sing Sing prison. That damn kid. That goddamn kid.*

It was time to go. He looked at the parcel. It was addressed to Pat Wilson in 5C. "Dammit," he whispered.

"I'm gonna leave this on the stoop." Pat liked to talk. He talked all kinds of stuff. He liked to hear himself talk. It was a nightmare. Pat never listened to your response to what he said, he would just continue on about this and that. His son was his favorite topic. There was no time now for Pat or his stories.

"I wish I knew what time it was," whispered the postman. His head darted around. There was no good option.

"I'm leaving this here." He compromised and bent down to place the parcel on the hall floor instead of outside on the stoop. That felt good. Someone would be along soon enough to give it to Pat Wilson. Let *them* hear his never ending monologue.

As he leaned down, the sleeve on his left arm rode up and the watch his son gave him became visible. It still read the wrong time. The watch remained a relic from a time that was right with his boy. The postman stood back up with the parcel in hand. He felt bad. He rang the bell.

The door buzzed almost immediately. A voice cracked through the intercom and asked who it was. Before he could answer, the door became free and the postman walked through the entrance and hollered up the stairs.

"Pat, have a package for you down here!"

The footsteps were already descending from the fifth floor. "Coming down, just wait right there! When you rang I was in the middle of making breakfast, omelets, and forgot to add the cheese to the eggs and you know what? It was so funny to see me running to the fridge and get the cheese into the pan before I flipped the omelet but somehow I made it. It's the perfect omelet. I left it on the warmer so that when I got back up there I could eat with my son."

Here it comes, thought the postman. "Well, that's all right Pat, I don't want to keep you from your eggs. Just didn't want to leave this thing out in the open so I thought I'd ring...."

"Ya know, Frankie will only eat eggs with cheese and only with me! It's our routine every morning! Breakfast and baseball stats, stretches first, of course! Have to keep the limbs limber." Pat's feet thudded on the second-floor landing as he grabbed the wooden paint-chipped railing at the top of the staircase. "I say it every day: my boy is gonna be a baseball star!"

"Pat, the package.... You don't need to sign." The postman held the brown, boxed parcel out in front of him; his back foot cheating toward the glass door. Pat gingerly descended the final flight of stairs to the black-and-white checkered landing. He leaned on the banister as he spoke.

"You ever see him throw?"

"Throw?"

"Yeah."

"Who? Your son?"

"He throws heat, a baby curve, a sinker, a screw ball—he throws them all."

"Wow. I can leave this on the bottom step for you, Pat. I have a ton of mail to get to today."

"He doesn't throw a proper curve; of course, I don't want to hurt that arm. He is bound for the Bigs."

The postman nodded, smiled, and turned away. The urge to somersault down the stoop and onto the free, quiet street came to his mind. Anything, any way to find the best path to escape and beat the traffic to Sing Sing prison; a prison that, despite who was behind the two-way glass, a father and son would always remain. Ringing the doorbell was a mistake. Thinking with the heart was a mistake. Wearing the watch was a mistake. Pat was still halfway up the staircase when he called to him.

"You look like you have a son—does he play ball?"

The postman looked at his watch and frowned. "I don't have a son. Don't forget your package." He placed the parcel on the ground, exited through the glass door, and almost slipped down the stoop; almost.

Pat shrugged and picked up the parcel. He brought the box close to his face and knew exactly what it was once he felt its weight and sniffed the worked leather on the cardboard of the parcel. It was the Rawlings brown leather infielder's glove he purchased for his son for the coming baseball season. Born only a few months before and shipped directly to his address, it was to be Frankie's new glove. It was like

Christmas during springtime when the new mitt arrived. Pat hugged the box and ascended the staircase like a cat, his hands yanking on the banister to give him more momentum back to the fifth floor. He couldn't wait to open it up, handle the glove, and get it ready for Frankie. "Working the mitt" is what he called it. The steps to working the mitt were as follows: oil and spit in the pocket of the mitt nightly, throw a hardball into the pocket over and over until the leather is almost putty and the palm of the hand stung like an angry swarm of bees, kiss the net of the glove and pet it often so it would always think of you kindly when those hot-shot ground balls came your way, and sleep with it next to your pillow so it might grow into the scalp and teach the brain how to make catches like Roberto Clemente. These things were crucial and necessary; a rite of passage for any boy to intake and process if he were to make it to the Show.

"And my boy is gonna be a baseball star!" He shouted into the sixth floor and skylight above as he crossed the hall to his apartment door. His voice echoed through the high ceiling and open halls. Pat looked around to see if anyone would come out to check out the commotion. Nothing stirred. Not even a mouse.

"A star, a baseball star!" he shouted again, this time down the five flights to the ground-floor lobby. There was barely an echo. Pat hugged the parcel close to his face again and looked down. The doormat read, "Father and Son's Place. Gonna Be Dirty Anyways So Don't Wipe!'" Pat stared at the mat. He wiped his shoes carefully and slowly pushed the door open. The bolt and latch clicked into place immediately after the door shut.

The apartment was filled with the hot scent of eggs and maple-cured bacon. The breakfast sat atop a hot plate warming on the stove. The stove was immaculate, almost preserved; not a drop of grease, salt grain, or pepper flake could be found anywhere around the burners. Pat prayed often and thought about the synergy of cleanliness and godliness and its importance on how if practiced correctly with a steady stream of ground balls his son might perform gracefully on the baseball diamond. Yes, baseball. Breakfast was secondary to the baseball mitt inside the brown parcel.

In the apartment now, Pat hurried over to the junk drawer of the curio cabinet. It was an antique and took up too much room in the four-and-half room railroad apartment. Yet he kept it dusted and polished most of the time. The curio had always been a weird thing in Pat's life. It was presented to him and his wife on their wedding day by his now-late grandmother. Not at a reception, but at the church. She had it timed magnificently: the cabinet was brought via moving truck to St. Aloysius and carted up the front church steps on a hand truck, wheeled down the aisle and straight to the holy altar after Pat had finished giving his bride the post-vow kiss. Two moving men waited for a tip and frowned when Pat shrugged and told him his pockets were empty. He felt they would understand, given the circumstances. They didn't; one of the moving men kicked the curio as he exited the church. Pat's grandmother came forward and gave some speech about the cabinet's meaning to the family and how it cost two hundred and forty dollars to construct. A half-applause came when the speech was over, but no one truly knew what to do after a speech about a curio cabinet that just been delivered to a church immediately after a wedding, so that wasn't too odd. Then it got odd again. At his grandmother's insistence, Pat and his new bride posed for a picture with the piece of furniture, turned and posed together at the altar with the curio behind them, and walked down the rest of the aisle. The curio stood tall and faced the gathering. No one moved. The priest spoke—"Let us go in peace"—and quickly exited out of the side door. All family members and guests waited their turn and followed each other down the maroon carpet. Then those odd folks from the neighborhood who just liked to attend weddings and stand in the back of the church followed next. Rice was thrown as Pat and his bride waved and got into the waiting white town car. The car honked and drove off; movie film images of white rice thrown and pantomime cheers through rolled-up, black-tint windows filled the sunlit Friday February afternoon. The curio cabinet remained at the church's altar through the weekend. The bizarreness continued as the church just had daily mass around it. One priest gave a homily and incorporated the curio cabinet into the moral. The shit really hit the fan when monsignor refused to pay for the cabinet to be moved off the altar and returned to Pat Wilson's house. Pat had it shipped home Monday at dawn after a threatening phone call came after Father Guy's last mass Sunday evening. Pat placed it upright, polished the wood, and both he and his bride filled its drawers and cabinets until they fell asleep. His grandmother died the following Tuesday morning. It all held a purpose in the end: the curio drawer held the scissors that would open the parcel. *Yes, everything had purpose and meaning*, he thought.

Pat cut the tape away from the edges with the scissors and ripped the box open. The leather scent overtook the room. Immediately he saw a vision of Pete Rose tipping his hat to the crowd after his 4192nd hit. He turned to his sons closed bedroom door. "Frankie! Got your glove, and boy is it a beaut!" The glove didn't fit Pat's hand, but he took to flapping it open and closed with his two fingers that fit. The leather scent cemented itself on his forearm and the Rawlings logo in gold script caught his eye. His boy was gonna be a star.

"Hey, get out here and see this thing! I have a hardball that we could use to work the pouch and belly of the mitt! Man, it's gonna be great out there today. The eggs and bacon are hot, so get out here and eat. I'm having mine!" Pat dished out some of the eggs on his plate, leaving room for three or four bacon slices. He made an even dozen. He snuck one before he plated his son's food. He still held the Rawlings glove in one hand.

"Getting cold!" Pat snuck another bacon strip. The bedroom door stayed quiet and closed. He laughed to himself. "You know they called Pete Rose Charlie Hustle? Number fourteen, Frankie, he hustled no matter what. You have to love a guy like that. All muscle, no hesitation. Hey, here's your mitt!" Pat flung the Rawlings glove at the middle of the door and it bounced off, spinning on the floor.

The bedroom door stayed silent. Pat rolled his eggs around on his plate and smiled.

"Pete Rose...ahem, I mean Charlie Hustle...would make the game, hell, even the practice if he were dead." The bacon crunched under his teeth and Pat laughed. "That's the kind of hustle I want from you, Frankie. Clemente, Rose,

Gwynn—those are the boys you can be like. Batters, ballers, and let me tell you, the competition around here, ahhhh, don't worry about them, son. You have got them beat with your cleats and your batting gloves. Your stance." Pat walked around and put an imaginary bat to the back of his shoulders. It hung and sung on an imaginary wind.

"The ground balls and the pop flys. You yell , 'I got it I got it' and all will fade back, my boy." Pat moved around the kitchen and immediately the tin ceiling became a blue, ballfield sky. The white hardball came down into the pouch of Pat's imaginary glove like Rickey Henderson patrolling the same way in a shallow centerfield.

"Oh, here's an easy one: the way you take a sip from the water fountain and the fans. Don't you worry about that any. It's all in how you smile and make good with the press. You and this Rawlings glove. Or another glove. It doesn't matter. As long as you're catching fly balls! And another thing, don't you worry about the rest, I am going to teach you how it's done."

Silence.

"But you have to get up, buddy, and get going, come on!"

Silence.

"I made breakfast, buddy, and your brand new leather Rawlings glove came in the mail for you to use."

Silence.

"We can work it in together."

Silence.

"You can work it in if you want to. Is that better?"

Silence.

"Getting cold, Frankie!"

Silence.

Pat pounded the table with his fists and the forks and knives clanked together. The banging continued louder now and his hands bounced rhythmically on top of the set-out silverware. "Hustle," he mumbled. Each time hands planted onto the table harder, truer. The blows shook the table, forcing the bacon on his son's plate to fall limply to the floor, the runny eggs barely clinging to the fake porcelain edge. Pat stopped. His hands trembled. Frankie's bedroom door remained closed and quiet. A low rumble came from below his feet now; he could hear the tenants below yelling, "Stop that banging you asshole" through the thinly uncarpeted floorboards.

Pat picked the fork back up and finished his eggs. His bacon was long gone, the table short and empty. Coffee that he had brewed kept itself warm in a red travel mug that read "Baseball Dad" in faded white print across its front. He took a long, slow sip of it and set it down on the table. Pat refused to look at the door anymore, but used the fork to move the egg back onto his son's breakfast plate; it slid back and pooled in the middle. The fallen bacon stared back up at him from the kitchen floor and Pat reached down and placed it neatly next to the egg.

Frankie's bedroom door stayed closed and silent. *Maybe he isn't hungry*, Pat thought.

He pushed his seat away from the table and walked to the bedroom door, his hand wrapped slowly around the old brass doorknob, gripping it tightly. The urge to turn and push the door open came and went like always. There was no use waiting, Frankie would be Pete Rose when he was good and ready. His hand released the doorknob and reached for the blue jacket that had "Coach" embroidered in white small script across the right breast. It barely fit as he tried to close the button snaps.

"Frankie, I am going to head down to the park. You just come out and get to those eggs when you're ready, okay? They are still warm and I left you bacon too! Okay? I've got your glove and the hardball so don't worry. Oh! Don't forget to stretch, buddy, hands to toes and hands on hammies, remember?" Pat reached down and did both stretches. His back felt a pinch on the way up and he winced and coughed. He hadn't stretched since last summer.

Baseball. That is what mattered. He grabbed the glove and ball and unbolted the front door.

"See you there, Frankie!" Pat didn't wait for an answer, but hurried down the hall into the stairwell. His footsteps echoed deep into the bottom-floor landing; they seeped below the cracks of the 1940 tile pattern and then past the cellar door, pooling next to the half-dead burner and the indoor sewer drain before fading away into the East River. Good. Everything ended up there anyway.

⅏

Ms. Virginia Madre held the metal guardrail and limped down the stoop. She hated walking. She hated moving. It was the phone call that had gotten her upright. She hated phone calls. The call was from the Russian in Brighton Beach. The bastard owned the apartment building; it was left to him by his parents in a contested will, one that he contested because he did not want the responsibility of owning or selling the property. In the end he inherited the lot. The Russian arrived one day and asked the tenants to gather in the stairwell. He told them he would not sell the building if they wouldn't break anything or make any trouble. All he asked was that they deliver the rent money at the end of the month. They could get it to him by the fifth of the month the latest. The tenants asked for his phone number in case of any emergency. He told them to call 911. Before leaving, he reiterated he wanted the rent by the fifth. That was all he wanted. All Ms. Madre wanted was her television and arm chair.

She reached the bottom of the stoop and stopped. The fog had finally begun to give way, letting in a little sun onto the bottom stair. Ms. Madre let her hand warm in the light. Here she would wait. The Russian from Brighton was on his way over to collect the rent as the calendar was well past the fifth and she hadn't sent the check to him yet, but she couldn't even had she wanted to. The pension provided to her was only at half salary now that Harry had passed away. The pension check was late. It was always late. Harry's company had slid back financially and was paying debts; all kinds of debt: life debt, loan debt, creditors debt, son-of-a-bitching debt. That wasn't all. The social security money she had taken too early wouldn't be enough to cover much of anything, let alone late rent. Nine hundred and fifty dollars' worth of rent. A one-bedroom apartment with bad views of a blighted backyard complete with bad plumbing. Son-of-a-bitching rent. Worse? The mailman wasn't by the block yesterday either. Neighbors gossiped about it on their stoops and across airshafts.

She hated Harry and debt and the son-of-a-bitching rent. *Where was the goddamn postman?* she thought.

"Ms. Madre, a cup of Sanka for you?" Telly held out the white mug in front of Ms. Madre's eyes. She liked Sanka.

"Yes, thank you."

Telly crouched low and sat down on the wet stoop.

"The stoop is wet, Telly, don't sit there."

"Ahh, it will dry off. I like sitting here."

Ms. Madre shrugged.

Telly looked around and sipped his own cup of Sanka. "Some fog out there, right? We never get fog like this! It is so eerie."

Ms. Madre brought the cup to her lips and turned her head to the right. No postman in sight. "You see or seen the postman, Telly?"

"Nope, be here soon, I hope. I heard some of the neighbors squawking that he didn't come yesterday either."

Ms. Madre sipped her Sanka. "He'll be here today."

"You hear a gunshot a little bit ago, Ms. Madre? I could've sworn I heard one."

"No. I was watching the television."

"It was loud."

"I keep the television loud."

"I almost called the police."

Ms. Madre turned her head to the left. Her eyes strained. "Why would you do something like that?"

"So the police would come and check it out, you know, to protect us."

No postman in sight. No nothing. Maybe it was the fog. It still hung around despite the emerging sun. Her eyes weren't what they used to be.

"They get calls like that all the time. They won't be coming around here for that. They didn't even come around when Mrs. Demeri was robbed and had a heart attack right down the street."

Telly laughed. "Yeah, they did!"

"Don't laugh at that. A woman died." Ms. Madre looked off into the fog. "They came. They came after she had died. Let me tell you, that *is* not going to happen to me."

A car turned down the block and roared up the street. Ms. Madre hated the sound; it grated on her worse than Jehovah's Witnesses pounding at the front door midday, midweek. She'd just as well turn the television volume up to one hundred and put her finger tips in her ears than hear that sort of racket. The car slowed when it got close to the apartment building. Ms. Madre froze. Perhaps it was the Russian. No, it was too soon. She had no rent money to give. All she had was a cup of Sanka. It wasn't even hot anymore.

"Telly, who is in that car?"

"Which one, Ms. Madre?"

"The one coming up the block, Telly."

Telly squinted. "To tell you the truth, I don't know."

The car slowed midway.

"Is it a man or woman?"

"Oh, looks like a man."

"Young or old?"

"Looks young."

"Does he look stupid?"

"Christ I don't know—they all do, Ms. Madre."

"Does he look really confused and stupid like he doesn't know what apartment building he is looking for?"

Telly didn't answer as the car pulled up alongside their apartment and then rolled on. The slow roll came to a stop and brake lights shone a bright red into the evaporating fog on the street. Telly sipped his Sanka while Ms. Madre waited for the car to be shifted into reverse. It didn't happen. In an instant, the horn honked once and a young girl bounced out of the door just a quarter way down the street from the stoop where Telly and Ms. Madre stood. She was dressed to be undressed. When the front passenger door slammed, the car sped off. Ms. Madre sighed. It was then that the fog lifted and Telly turned and grabbed Ms. Madre's hand. It was shaking.

"Who are you waiting for, Ms. Madre?"

She didn't answer.

"The Russian?"

She nodded.

"You didn't pay the rent yet?"

Ms. Madre didn't answer but looked around her; the empty street looked even emptier now. The sidewalk even seemed longer. The sky, now visible, seemed larger than before. She held no jurisdiction on any of this. The Russian was at full speed in his cruiser racing toward Cypress Avenue. The postman carrying precious postage was nowhere to be seen. This was a race against time. The Sanka in her cup was cold. Telly took her hand.

"Don't you worry. The postman is bound to come soon. And if he doesn't, well, the Russian will just have to understand that these sort of things happen."

"I hate the Russian."

"That's fair, we all do."

"I wish Harry were still here, Telly."

"I know."

"Do you?"

"He isn't and he won't be coming back, Ms. Madre."

"I hate Harry."

"I could make a fresh pot of coffee if you like? Look down there, some kids are playing in the street."

Ms. Madre looked and shook her head. "Sanka, Telly."

Telly came close to her ear. "No more Sanka or no more kids?"

"I need my check. Where is the postman, goddammit?"

Telly looked up. From the distance he could see a figure coming down the street, quick-paced and splashing in the leftover rain pooled on the sidewalk. It wasn't the postman. He was walking too fast for that.

"Someone's coming, Ms. Madre."

"Is it the mailman?"

"I don't think so."

Ms. Madre looked and squinted. The figure made sense once the arm came up and waved. The voice followed.

"Hey guys, happy Sunday!"

Telly looked to Ms. Madre and shrugged his shoulders. She didn't move. Telly shook her arm.

"Who is that guy?"

"Pat."

"Pat?"

"Yes. Pat."

"I don't know Pat."

Ms. Madre looked the other way. The postman was absent from that direction as well. She turned back to Telly. "Pat Wilson."

"Pat Wilson….Pat Wil…oh, Coach Wilson."

"Used to be. Fifteen years ago."

"He's not a coach anymore?"

"He thinks he is."

"You think he isn't?"

"He's not anymore."

"Everyone around here calls him Coach Wilson."

Ms. Madre snapped her fingers before she spoke. "Everyone around here still calls Met Food Supermarket 'Bohack's' because that's what it was called twenty years ago. Get it?"

"Yeah. I loved Bohack's."

Ms. Madre smiled. "It's gone, don't love it anymore."

"Does he still call himself coach?"

"Who cares?"

Pat arrived at the stoop and stopped. He was slightly out of reach.

"Ms. Madre, great day, isn't it? How are you?"

Ms. Madre nodded and sipped the cold Sanka. Pat didn't notice, he had already taken the hardball out of his mitt and threw it back hard into the leather pouch. The leather snapped. Telly extended his hand out as he spoke.

"I'm Telly, Telly Jones—Ms. Madre says…." Telly noticed Pat's jacket read coach. "Aren't you a coach?"

Pat threw the hardball up in the air high. It caught a few leaves of the tree overhead before coming down and settling in the pouch of the glove. He turned to Telly.

"I coach baseball. Only one player. Madre knows."

Telly looked at Ms. Madre. She stared straight down. Church bells chimed in the distance.

"Who do you coach, man?"

"Madre, you know! The best heater, slow curve, sinker, funny ball in the land. You know." A rush of a car down the street put the thought of the Russian back in her mind. Ms. Madre kept her head low. Pat threw the ball up high and caught it again. "My son will be along soon, he's finishing up breakfast."

Telly looked at Ms. Madre. "You coach your son?"

"Oh, he's a bugger on the field. Arm like Strawberry. Pete Rose hustle. This glove right here, the one I was catching those fly balls in, well, it is his and we are going to work it out in a little bit. Ms. Madre, I ever tell you about the stance I taught him?"

Ms. Madre looked up and half smiled as the church bells continued their song. She knew where this was going. "Tell me again, Pat."

"Frankie knows the stance of all of his heroes, well, they were my heroes, but they became his heroes too and he practiced in the front near the stoop, remember, Madre?" Pat jumped into position, arms raised in a batting stance set to swing for the parking lot. "I coached him this way, uh...."

"I'm Telly."

"Sorry. I coached him this way, Telly. Showed him the best batting stances and the best way to pivot the foot when fielding. He won an all-star trophy in sixth grade."

"Every kid wins a trophy at that age."

"Did you, Telly?"

"Yes."

"You must be mistaken because not every kid wins a trophy. My son, he won THE trophy."

"I won a trophy in sixth grade, I think."

"Frankie won that trophy and he and I worked out all summer long throwing hardballs across the fields near Grover Cleveland High School—where I was an all-star too!" Pat threw the ball into the pit of the mitt a few times over to reinforce the memory to himself. "I was an all-star too, just like you, buddy…." His voice trailed off under his breath into a whisper.

Ms. Madre listened. The church bells rang in succession: one, two, three….

"And Frankie and I would go to the Farmer's Oval to practice fly balls midday because nobody was there except the handball players and the vagabonds who wanted to sleep off last evening's suds. You know them: the ones that lay asleep in the green manicured grass like a human obstacle course. Frankie loved it. I loved it. Throwing the ball up high near where I thought the tramps would lay so that Frankie could stand over them, still keep his eye keen on the ball as it landed in his mitt that was hovering a foot off of the drunks face. No worse for the wear, Frankie would tip his cap to the sleeping beauty and send the ball back to me in on swoop. Mickey fucking Mantle."

Telly smiled. "Mickey Mantle."

Pat went on. "After the fly ball routine, I'd get him to the plate. He needed to hit a few. So he'd choke up on the wooden bat. That's right, a wooden bat! I didn't let my kid swing with no metal thing. He'd stand there at the plate, like Harmon Killerbrew, the Killerrrrr…and wait for my deep-dish pizza pitch. You should've seen him belt those balls. They sailed and sailed. One landed on another ball field where other kids were playing once. They thought it

76

was the ball to their game at first. Nope. It was Frankie, the all-star. My son could swing and hit."

Telly patted Pat's shoulder. "Wow, I can't wait to meet this kid!"

The bells continued: four, five, six, seven.

Pat shook his head. "What?"

"Your son, I can't wait to meet him."

"Yeah, well…." Pat looked around. It all seemed unfamiliar now. His voice was shaky. "Uh, he's meeting me at the field, so."

Telly jumped up and down. "Baseball season is right around the corner!"

"Yeah, well, yeah…it's right around the corner." Pat tucked the hardball into the undersized mitt. It still didn't fit his hand. It was made for a little boy. It was made for Frankie. Ms. Madre tried to yank on Telly's arm to get his attention but he was out of reach. Telly thought he could be a coach now too. Maybe he could even help coach Frankie.

"Yeah, Pat, you gotta get that boy to practice! He needs all the fly balls, groundballs, and dirt slides a boy can get."

Pat looked at the glove. The leather scent was strong now, a stench almost. The urge to dig a six-foot hole and bury the glove came over him. It happened every spring but he didn't dig a hole nor place anything down inside it. It was summer now. Frankie's laughter echoed throughout his head as he rubbed the mitt across his cheek; the leather scent still strong. It felt like home. It felt whole. Pat looked down the street toward his home. Ms. Madre looked in the same direction. No Frankie. No postman. Nothing. Both would have to go on beyond the onset of midday, dusk, twilight, night, straight through midnight and wait. The neverending waiting room of Cypress Avenue.

Baseball. Baseball is all that mattered.

"I better be going, Ms. Madre. Have a good day."

Ms. Madre nodded. Pat tucked the mitt under his arms and fast-walked down the sidewalk in the direction of the ball field.

The belling kept on: eight, nine, ten, eleven, twelve.

"Can't wait to see your boy on the field, Pat! Take care," Telly waved and turned to Ms. Madre and tapped her on the shoulder.

"Such a nice guy, so glad I got to meet him."

"Oh?"

"Yes. He is all about that boy, huh?"

"Yes."

"Must be some kid."

There was no answer from Ms. Madre. Telly laughed to himself when she didn't respond.

"What, is his son a bad kid or something?"

Ms. Madre turned her head again and looked down the street in the direction where the postman ought to appear from. "No, he isn't a bad kid."

"So why didn't you say anything about him? Sounds like you knew him."

"Pat likes to go on about his son; sometimes he doesn't listen to anyone else, and the stories last too long."

"Oh. But are they true?"

"Yes."

"It's funny. The talk has always been about his kid when it comes to baseball. I never seen him play. I don't think he plays in my nephew's school."

Ms. Madre checked her watch. Telly nudged her again.

"Well, why don't we go see them throw the ball around after the postman drops by? I could use a day out in the park. You could too. His kid sounds amazing."

"I am going back upstairs and into my easy chair at once…if I can pay the Russian the rent."

"I am going to go down there and watch them by myself then."

"You won't see him there, Telly." Ms. Madre gave into her legs and sat down on the second-to-last step on the stoop. The rain still settled there was sucked into the threads of her muumuu. The Sanka grounds darkened the bottom of the mug.

Telly shook his head in confusion. "Why won't I see him there? Oh, and you need another cup, Ms. Madre?"

"Yes. But, wait a minute."

Telly turned and waited. A wind kicked up and a police siren rang.

"Last time I saw his son was eleven years ago. Greenwood Cemetery."

&

The postman descended the stoop. He cursed under his breath. His knees and ankle bones cursed too. His hands, no different. It was a steady stream of up down, run wait, stop check, file fold, place slot, check again. He was nothing but a government butler for endless unneeded paper correspondence. At the bottom of the stoop sat his blue carriage. The blue lost some of its hue slightly to rain and snow, but it was still a solid piece he could lean on during the day.

He was tired now. Lower back and leg pain as always, but a fatigue came over him; a future fatigue not yet experienced which the highway driving was going to provide. It was an anxiety fatigue, an irrational fatigue. It settled in the gut and weighed his toes down, pressing the black canvas sneakers he'd worn diligently since he was seventeen to the lowest point of the ground. Those sneakers fit like slippers now. He longed for home.

The church bells toned. The postman paused. Time? What time was it? He looked to his watch. *Son-of-a-bitching thing,* he thought. The belling continued and he counted each slowly. Twelve chimes came and went. Noon. Son of a bitch, it was noon.

The postman looked down into his carrier and surveyed the sea of letters and magazines. The route was far from finished; it wouldn't be complete for hours. He didn't have hours. Traffic built itself in minutes. He thumbed through the bag watching each name, each address, each postage stamp slip by. How many would lose this day he wouldn't know. He didn't care. He wouldn't lose on the Taconic Parkway. Not this day.

He pushed the carrier forward and it rolled down the sidewalk toward Cypress Avenue. The postman walked in the opposite direction.

they break our legs and give us crutches

he thing about walking down the long, tan-colored concrete sidewalks of Cypress Avenue, no matter the time of day, was that a man could feel much like a ghost ship at night adrift on an open ocean. I liked it that way. It was easy to mutter under your breath or even hold lengthy, back-and-forth conversations out loud while passing by seas of stoops and open storefronts. I'd come across a person now and again along the way, but I kept the conversation going. It didn't matter much. Most of the people hanging around the Avenue didn't speak any English, unless it had to do with money or drugs.

These days, there was a steady flow of young adults moving in and out of the neighborhood. I didn't mind change. I did mind this special new breed of kid, though; every portion of their adult lives was funded and supplemented by Mommy or Daddy to afford these twentysomethings plenty of time to sit around and smoke dope, dress like dopes, eat like dopes, and talk like dopes, while masquerading around as the best and brightest of the artistic world. Easy to spot and deal with, viciously if needed. I liked that too. I often took to muttering loudly when passing them on the street. They never knew what to make of me, so they just kept quiet. It was perfect: no one knew what I was saying; I didn't know nor care what they were saying, and I was surrounded by dopes. All I wanted to do was cast my line and fish.

And that's just what I had done.

The sight of my fingernails stained pink and red right to the cuticles with the day's catch kept the thought of the dopes out at sea with the rest of the live bait.

The bridges, the seas, the boroughs between: fifty years old and I still am most at ease standing at the edge of a jetty with a pole and baited hook in one hand, Ma's heart in the other, watching the tide come and go. Sometimes I'd sit cross-legged on the warm wood boards of an ocean-worn pier. The barnacles that clung to the underbelly would come to light when the tide was out just far enough, and that's when I'd wave to them. *Good morning, barnacles, what ocean secrets do you have for me this day?* They whispered to me about a fleet of horseshoe crabs crashing the beach when the tide returned later that evening. I would wait for those horseshoe crabs; those prehistoric blue-blooded, black-bodied little buggers. They came as the sun sweated away over the horizon, the end to a day's long catch. The beach trapped them and there they would sit, enduring the taunts of little kids throwing rocks or poking them with sticks when they got too close. I'd set my pole in the sand tight and run over to chase away those bastard kids. They called me the horseshoe crab horseshit man. I'd throw worms and fish guts at them. It was a day at the beach for all. I'd have hours to go before that fun, however. It was then I'd pay close attention to the movements of my pole between sips of scotch and nibbles of saltwater taffy. Fifty years old and I still like my saltwater taffy. Most times I'd go into a daydream or just listen to the solitary gulls call across the spread of the beach. I'd liken it to driving and arriving at a destination and not remembering exactly what happened during the drive. You knew you had driven somewhere, you just didn't know how. It was then that my line would tug a little and I knew I either had a bluefish or a striper or even if I were sitting in the right spot at the first part of dawn, the possibility of a bite from a yellowfin tuna that was just passing through New York Harbor. It happened before. After a fifteen-minute fight, Ma and I ate tuna steaks that night. What an angry, strong little fishy. Once skinned and filleted, Ma would panfry them in salted Breakstone's butter, cracked pepper, shallots, and capers. She even opened a bottle of French wine. I was used to the ten-dollar back alley kind. She was too, but that night we dined like the others who lived across the bridge in the upper part of Manhattan Island.

Ma is seventy-five. I used to think that was prehistoric when I was a boy; prehistoric like the dopey horseshoe crab. Some nights I'd cry in her arms about her getting old and one day going to heaven the way Papa had gone and done years before. Ma made me feel better about getting old. She likened it to fishing. She likened almost everything to fishing. "Earl," she'd say. "Getting old ain't easy, but think of it like the worm waiting on the edge of your hook out in that big great ocean. The worm knows something is coming;

he doesn't know exactly what, but he can hang there and watch the beauty of the reef and the heavenly way the light reflects in the ocean current and think: I am alive. He could be seven minutes or seventy years old, but there he is, on that hook, not knowing when or where that fish might come to take him away, but living. Alive. Just like me. And you, baby blue."

My best thought of Ma was her sitting and waiting for me at the apartment. She'd always be there. I often told myself that.

We—our family—had lived on Cypress Avenue since the first apartment buildings had gone up a hundred years or so ago. Ma and I were the natives here. Her family had lived in the same apartment since the thirties and, before her, their parents and grandparents and their parents lived in a building almost directly across the street that had since burned down. Had the building not burned away, chances are I'd be standing in the same spot where my great-great-grandpa and great-great-uncle probably stood and undoubtedly drank port while talking about casting lines. Our family hated moving. They hated change. It's the "birds of the same feather" thing when it comes to me. I gave everything and everyone a fair shake, but I never accepted change.

We had always lived in the shadow of the city's bridges, farmed the county and island's seas, and stayed within the limits and length of Cypress Avenue. I always would. Ma too. Well, maybe until the building burned down.

The rain had come and gone since I descended the subway stairwell and boarded the A train at the Broad Channel stop.

It was an even twelve blocks from the elevated M train to the apartment, so that was good. I could walk it blindfolded. It had been a long morning and my back was starting to feel a little stiff. The city made bus service limited down Cypress Avenue years ago in a cost-cutting measure to offset another cost-cutting measure in Forest Hills Gardens. I shifted the weight of my poles from my right shoulder to the left and stretched out my back a bit. The muscle that had cramped up in my shoulder blade spasmed, then slowly released. It felt a little better but still not great. It was nothing a taste of scotch and a shot of Atlantic Ocean saltwater couldn't heal. I think I still have a little of the twelve-year bottle of the Grand Macnish scotch left over in the cooler.

No, I don't.

That drunk Tina finished the last of it while I gutted the fish. And I can't be mad about it; I told her she could. Two hours of her nonstop narrative about her girlfriends and her roommates and her boss forced my hand. I had the fillet knife in one hand and the Macnish in the other. The fish had to be gutted and cleaned before we left the pier. Tina got the Macnish. At least it shut her up for twenty minutes.

I put the cooler down and flipped the lid. One, two, five, eight...eight fish on ice and two cups of saltwater for them to soak in the sink once I get home. Ma and I were going to eat good tonight.

"Woah, nice catch, man!"

I looked up. It was one of the dopes. I should have never stopped here. I knew there was no scotch left in the cooler but I just had to look anyway. Truth is, I liked looking at the fish, too. They were beautiful white-and-gold stripers—all around twelve pounds or so. A magnificent fish that liked the fight and would only allow you to reel it in when it knew you and your tired arms were ready for another drink. Its perfect form would be revealed when it broke the surface to face your outstretched hand; ocean wet and flapping midair on your hook and line. There he hung and waited against the steel pole for his finale, a Jesus of the sea. I had never seen such beauty like that before the first time I casted a line into the blue and green deep.

"Man, you hear me?"

Then there was the dope. I looked him over. Usual story: he was dressed in red paint-stained sweat pants, black military-style boots laced to the top of the tongue, and a white t-shirt that read GLAM in hot pink across the chest. The attire was completed with a stupid fedora hat and movie-star sunglasses.

I didn't answer him but kept my head down closer to the cooler. The scent of salt water and fresh cold bass was heavenly. Perhaps he would think me crazy and walk in the opposite direction of Cypress Avenue that I was headed down. I turned my head away now and fiddled with the bottom of the cooler, pretending to work on it. The tan concrete sidewalks looked darker since the rain soaked them an hour ago. I looked back. There was the black boot. The dope was still standing there.

"Hello, bro, man, you okay?"

I had to answer. I looked up at him. "What?"

"You a fisherman?"

I closed the lid of the cooler and stood up. I still held my poles. "Am I a what?"

"Are you a fisherman?"

I stared the length of my poles for a moment before I answered.

"What's it look like?"

"Well, I'd guess that you are a fisherman."

"You'd guess?"

"Yes"

"Yes?"

"Yeah"

"Yeah?"

"Yeah man, you must be a fisherman."

"You're goddamn right. Do you like to fish?"

"Yeah man, I do, I mean, I like to fish."

"Oh you like *to* fish. You should know the answer to this then." I threw the poles to the ground and they crashed on the front cellar gate.

"Hey, take it easy, man!" The dope backed up a bit. I could see the fear welling up inside him now, even behind the movie-star sunglasses. Those sunglasses didn't even protect his eyes; you could see right through the tint. What was their purpose? What was his purpose? I didn't know. I'd wager he didn't know either. A purposeless dope wasting my time about things I knew deep down he didn't care about.

I needed to get this over with and get the fish back home to Ma. I could hear and smell the salt and butter crackling in the cast iron pan.

"Here goes."

"Here what goes?"

"The question every fisherman should know the answer to."

"I'm not a fisherman, sir."

"I'm from a long line of fisherman and not to be fool-ed with."

"Okay, man."

"You said you liked my fish and you like to fish, did you not?"

"Yeah, but...."

The dope was getting under my skin now. "So, are you are a fisherman?"

"Hey, take it easy, I only meant that...."

"What are you, dope?"

"Take it easy man, take it easy."

"Give me an answer or your wallet."

The dope didn't react. Good. Onward.

"What does a bottle of scotch and a fillet knife have in common?"

The dope didn't answer.

"Every good angler knows the answer."

He looked at the fillet knife that was attached to my belt for the answer. I slid my hand over the handle.

"Every good angler knows...."

The dope turned and ran. He knew the answer. A young woman pushing a baby carriage had stopped to watch the action. I smiled at her. She mumbled something in Spanish and sped off in the same direction as the dope. Good, all clear ahead and no one in sight. I stretched my back again and reached down for the fishing poles. This time they would go back on my right shoulder. There was only five more blocks to go and there was plenty of scotch in the apartment. And Ma. That hot skillet, too.

The thing about Cypress Avenue is that you can be a ghost ship.

&

"Earl, is that you?"

"Yep Ma, I'm coming in."

"You don't have that drunk girl with you, do you?"

"Which drunk girl, Ma?"

"The old one. The one who you used to go with from the liquor store?"

"What liquor store?"

"Oh come on, the one down the street."

"Nunny's, Ma."

"Yeah, Nunny's. She with you?"

"No, Ma, just the fish."

"What's her name again?"

"Doesn't matter. I caught eight stripers, Ma."

"Goldie's her name, right Earl?"

"Yes, Ma."

"How many fish did you say you got?"

"I caught eight stripers today."

"Oh boy, that's good. I'll get the spices and things all ready for them. I want those fish to marinate a few hours before I put them in the oven. Wait, are they all cleaned up nice, Earl?"

"Yes, Ma."

"Okay good, I don't want them to get the kitchen all bloody because I just cleaned up here this morning. You set them on the counter. I will get my basin pan."

Ma scurried away into the dark end of the kitchen. It was always only half lit in there, a constant that started with my father when I was a boy. He was always talking about "saving the juice" to keep the electric down. I never saw the bills, so none of it mattered to me. It was one small lamp hanging over the kitchen table that could only handle a forty-watt light bulb. Ma hated white light bulbs, so she used an orange bulb in its place. That never bothered me at all. It bathed just a small section of the small kitchen in what always seemed to me to be like the glow of a street lamp. Ma hummed as she picked through the pots and pans and it was always the same song: Irving Berlin's *Blue Skies*. Nothing changed. There in the shadow of the orange glow in a white apron, her hair in bobby pins, humming *Blue Skies* in the kitchen that my father built for her almost twenty years ago.

"Oh boy, now where's the basin pan, Earl?"

"I don't know, Ma, I don't use the basin pan."

"I put it back right here. I know I did."

"Want me to look, Ma?"

"No, you just put the fish on the counter. You didn't bring that drunk girl, right? She's not waiting in the hall, is she?" Her head was deep in the cabinet and her voice echoed.

"Jesus, Mary, and Joseph, Ma…."

Ma's two cats Murphy and Sheeba darted across my feet and disappeared into the kitchen after her. I called to them but they didn't come back. Those two little dirtbags ignored everyone except for Ma. I called to them again; even though I couldn't see them, I knew they were there because I heard their purrs and Ma whispering "Okay okay, you wait here, babies" to them. They knew what the clanking cookware meant. They also knew what the scent coming from the cooler meant as well. They used to be my cats. I found them crying in an ashcan near the alley at the end of the street. I brought them home, cleaned them up, fed them fish guts, and let them sleep on top of my pillow at night. Seven years later they don't come when I call them. They're Ma's cats now. I didn't care for cats anymore anyway.

"Ma, you need help getting that thing out of there?"

"No no. you go inside and put on the TV. I am going to get the fish ready. Where'd you put the fish?"

"On the counter, Ma."

"On the counter?"

"Yes."

"Okay, I found the basin, so you go inside."

"Did you tape that program for me, Ma?"

"Yes, I did it last night. The tape is in the machine. It rewound itself after it was done recording. Just press play."

I left Ma in the kitchen and headed into the living room. My father's red leather easy chair still looked good and felt even better to sink into. Many an afternoon he would snooze there with the black-and-white television set on low volume as Ma hummed and drummed around the kitchen while making dinner or washing the dishes. They never spoke much, but they were happy. I looked at the chair. That would be me tonight.

The video tape was sticking out of the VCR. Ma labeled the front "A Night With Leroy Jenkins—San Antonio Texas 1974." I checked the grandfather clock. It was a large brown piece with gold trim and had been standing in the same spot since my father's father gifted it to the family one Christmas. It was big, in the way, and always thirty minutes slow—had been for years. It wasn't the clock, though. My father set and wound it that way. Ma wanted him up at 6:00 for dinner but he never fell asleep until 4:30. He wanted at least two hours of shuteye after work, and Ma wanted us seated, forks in hand, ready to say grace and eat directly at 6:00. So father set the grandfather clock back thirty minutes. Before Ma went to yell at him to wake and wash up, the first thing she'd do is look at the grandfather clock. The oven clock said 6:00, but the grandfather clock said 5:30. My mother was regularly confused and she never crossed my father, so she accepted that the time was actually 5:30 and left him alone in the red leather easy chair. I never knew the truth about the time until much later in life. During those days, however, I never made it to school on time nor ate dinner until 6:30.

It was now ten past 12:00 in the afternoon (11:40 on the old granddaddy). The video tape was sucked into the machine and automatically started playing. It was a black screen for now, but the tracking was off. I fiddled with that and raised the volume until the church pipe organ started coming through the television speakers. I looked up at the set. There he was: Leroy Jenkins.

Leroy Jenkins always reminded me of Elvis Presley at the end of his life: sweaty, dark cropped hair matted to his big white head like a helmet, and a voice complete with a half-Southern twang during his televised sermons. I heard it was an act he put on only when he visited the South. It mattered not. The son of a bitch could mesmerize any crowd. Ma loved him. I watched him because she asked me to. The television speakers cracked as the crowd roared and cheered while Leroy walked onto the stage.

"Praise Jesus," Ma said from the kitchen.

"Praise Jesus," Leroy echoed immediately after through the television set.

Ma loved church. She loved Jesus. She seemed to love Leroy Jenkins even more. It started to worsen after father passed away. I didn't care for it, but she seemed alive again in the daily congregation or by her lonesome in the back of the church lighting electric candles and slipping dollars bills into the prayer donation slot. Ma was easy to find; it was morning church and evening prayer, then watching the televangelists until dawn, and then on to sending away for free holy spring water that was certain to bring prosperity and endless hallelujahs. I didn't care much for it. I watched Leroy anyway. It was the bridge in my morning until the first race I could wager on at noon. My bookie banned me from all gambling until my fishing and my morning sermon was over after Ma paid him off; it was a condition of us still being "friends." I was just glad he still took my calls. I think he only did because he knew Ma would always pay the wager if I couldn't.

I sat in father's chair and Leroy Jenkins got underway:

> *Good morning. I want to tell you all how happy I am to be here today in San Antonio, Texas, with you all. (Amen!) That's right, I am here because I love you all. (Amen.) Amen, praise God. And I love people that really have stood with me and that I came here today—I just want to just tell you all, I love you. (We love you too! Amen.) You have all come to the crusade today because you have God and you know he will send you a miracle that*

*will change your life. (Amen.) That's right, Amen.
Now this lady right here, many a years ago, her
flesh was turning to stone (No, No.) and God killed
her, then she had cancer and God killed her again
(Thank you, Lord!), and so I looked around and
remembered, it had been years and years since I'd
seen her and here she is, still here through a miracle
of God! Amen! (Amen.) God said as your faith be,
your faith be unto you. (That's right.) God said ask,
and you shall receive, but seek—so the pathway, we
are all on the same pathway, the same direction, we
might have problems along the way, but God said
he will bring you through (Hallelujah!) and you
know, it won't be an easy walk but all that matters,
my friends, is what you become after you walk out
that door today! Amen! (Amen and hallelujah!)*

"Amen, Earl! Say Amen."

"Amen, Ma."

"Not to me, to God."

"Amen, God."

"That Goldie was around here looking for you the
other day."

I didn't respond.

"Earl, the Goldie girl…."

"Okay, Ma, I heard you."

"So answer me then."

"Amen, Ma."

"No, about Goldie."

"I heard you."

"You gotta set her straight, Earl. Listen to Pastor Jenkins, he knows about the devil and his temptations."

"I don't care about nothing but fishing and you, Ma."

"Are you listening to Pastor Jenkins?"

"I'm trying to, Ma."

"He knows about the devil."

I turned to the television. There was a close up of Leroy Jenkins with his hands raised over the head of an old man who was shaking on a set of crutches.

And this man right here, praise God, he is here and he knows about the word. (Amen.) What's your name, sir? John is his name, like the apostle John! God told me, you know what he said? (No.) They break our legs and give us crutches. Amen, that's right, Amen—John, they break our legs and give us crutches. Look at him right now, legs don't work anymore and leaning here shaking and crying on the remedy man can provide. You ready for what heaven can provide, John? (Amen, Hallelujah!) Are you ready, John, for what God can give you? (Amen! Praise God.) Take away those crutches; take them away! Look now, he is standing free, and, praise God, he is standing here before you and with love and full love of God. You didn't believe and now you know God is a healer. God has put his hand upon you and you can help others be other that hand anointed in front of God.

"Is he standing yet, Earl?"

"They break our legs and give us crutches," I whispered.

"It's the best part, him standing with Pastor Jenkins."

"Yeah, Ma."

"I gotta see! Don't fast forward, I gotta see!"

Ma came into the room and looked at the television. She reached into the front pocket of her apron and produced a small vile of water. The bottle was lit with television light as she held it to her face and smiled.

"Amen, Amen."

"Amen, Ma."

The old man stood up from the wheelchair and cried as he walked across the stage and into the arms of a man dressed in a suit standing next to Leroy Jenkins. The crowd roared and hollered at the stage. Leroy Jenkins held his hands out to them:

> *This is all possible because of the holy water vial that he received after writing me. This man is my partner in Christ. He has his legs, he has his future, and (Amen.) if he uses my holy water as point of contact, he can expect—what can you expect? Amen, listen to me, you can expect your medical bills to be taken care of by God. I hate when people say to me, "You look good for your age," I laugh and say that when I was born through the glory of God I had no teeth—that is true. But it is also true that when you get older you have no teeth, either. Nothing is too hard for the Lord. He's not gonna die, she's not gonna die (Hallelujah!) No, no, the death angel just walked away because none of you are gonna die. Not today. Amen!*

I looked at my hands. They were stained pink. I was a fisherman. Like Jesus and his merry men. The sea had given to me, I gave to Ma, the carousel spun, and we all went around it. In the end, Leroy Jenkins was right. They break our legs and give us crutches. Love? I get Goldie. I get Tina. I can't have either of them but they persist like a hangnail until they are gutted out. I get a neighborhood, polluted with the unemployable that are happy to be unemployed. My recompense is an alternative route around Cypress Avenue, the avenue of my ancestors. I have to slip and sneak through back alleys and side streets to get away from the privileged excrement. Then there's my father. The man leaned back and took a heart attack in the same chair I am sitting in now, watching the same television he watched baseball on and drank Rheingold beer in front of. Now Pastor Jenkins played the field on his set. Ma jumped up and down in the kitchen as the sermon on the VHS faded out and stopped.

"Amen!"

"Amen, Ma."

"Earl, you don't have that girl coming by, right? What's her name?"

"Which one, Ma?"

"The old one, Earl."

I looked at my hands again. The pink seem to darken into a blood red. "No, Ma, she isn't coming here. It's just you, me, and the fish."

"Okay, but if she shows up, I'm gonna break your legs."

"Okay, Ma."

The room grew quiet.

"Ma?"

"What?"

"Can I have a little of Leroy Jenkins miracle water?"

"Oh sure, here, use this one. I have plenty more put away in my bedroom."

Ma handed me the vial and bent close to my ear, "Amen, son," and patted me on the shoulder.

"You pray to God and Pastor Jenkins, Earl. You pray loud and true and the death angel will never get you. Just hold that miracle spring water tight." Ma turned and walked back into the kitchen calling after the cats. They meowed happily as they circled her feet. The faint hum of *Blue Skies* echoed across the apartment.

I tore open the vial and poured the water into my hands, rubbing them together as hard as I could. My stained hands stayed stained. I rubbed harder and looked heavenward.

"No death angels. Amen. Hallelujah." I whispered.

BOOK II

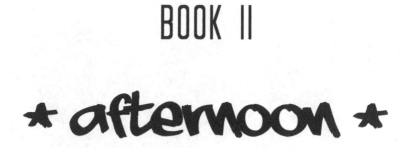

★ afternoon ★

daughters

Pip took his foot off the gas pedal and rolled the car down the avenue. There were no spaces to park—minus the illegal spot next to the defunct Johnny pump. Pip pulled in and brought the car to a stop. He shook Dezzy.

"Wake up, baby. Time to wake up and get out."

Dezzy slowly opened her eyes. She felt around; her hand grazed the cold buckle and slid across the length of the seat belt. There was a strange sense about her, not the usual feeling that came after the powder wore off; that feeling she could deal with and almost look forward to. This wasn't that. Dezzy had a name for that. The ache. She bit her lips and laughed. The ache meant she had made it through another go-around with the *stuff* in the Ridgewood ring. It meant she could again wash away that ache with lemon water, a soft gin fizz, a good talking to in the car rearview mirror, and a gallon of hot green tea—perhaps even an afternoon nap. Ms. Fixit, as Pip sometimes called her. Dezzy smiled when she thought about it.

"Hey, what are you doing? Wake up, Dezz."

Pip's voice startled her and she sat up quickly. Her hands felt around the front of the car for the usual suspects: keys to her apartment, keys to Sam Jean's apartment, pre-paid cell phone, the rest of the *stuff.* No stuff.

"Shit."

"Shit what?"

Dezzy looked at Pip and made a face. With a click she unbuckled herself, turned around, and scanned the backseat and the car floor. Empty. Well, not completely empty. The heavy scent of white linen car freshener rose from the multicolored scent trees that lined the back seats. They hung everywhere. The crazy bastard kept the car immaculate and Dezzy never knew why. She never asked, either.

"Why linen?" she whispered.

"I like linen; reminds me of my mom hanging the laundry on the clothesline when I was a kid. She always had those wooden clip things lying around the house.... What are they again?"

Dezzy laughed. "Clothespins?"

"Yeah, them. I used to play with them like they were toys. I was always losing those things. Mom would freak out when she found one laying on the floor or in my room under the bed."

Her laughter continued at his expense. "What would you play when you played with clothespins? Some kind of sexual game or something?"

Pip waved his hands at her. "Okay, go on, get out now. I have had enough of you."

Dezzy reached up and adjusted the rearview mirror toward her face. Heavy circles under her eyes and smeared mascara looked back. She fitted her hair into a ponytail and slipped the white hair band around the hair. Her hair needed a good brushing, so did her teeth, and she needed to get a little food in her. Dezzy had no money but her momma was working at Chicken Galore. Dezzy never liked going there; the cooks were always sweating and moaning in the kitchen area and her momma was always angry and yelling about something. But there would be food and even a little money, and she had to face her angry Puerto Rican momma sooner than later.

Pip tapped her arm the arm. "See you tomorrow?"

Dezzy turned to him. "I don't know. I have to get more money from Sam. Then I'll know."

"What do you do to get that money again?"

Dezzy shrugged.

"You're right, I don't want to know. Call me if you want. I'm only ten minutes away, baby."

Dezzy pulled the car door handle and pushed the door with her foot. "Right. See you."

The fog had somewhat lifted and the street was sunlit and quiet; Dezzy squinted and guessed it was probably around midafternoon. The strangeness she felt in Pip's car began to go away as she put one foot in front of the other. Dezzy didn't pay much attention to what direction she was headed in. The walk was fine; she took many of them when she was able. Sometimes she'd leave after breakfast and disappear down side street after side street, tumbling past bodegas and florists; sometimes she'd go into the McDonald's to use the bathroom, lock and jam the door and just sit there with her headphones on in the stall while the day manager yelled at her in Spanish. Some days Dezzy would leave the head-phones home, hit on the stuff, and just walk with her head looking toward the roofs of the apartment buildings.

Today it was that kind of day. She tilted her head up.

The Ridgewood apartment building tops were the bottom ceilings to the floors of heaven she thought.

"Heaven should be simple," she whispered. This wasn't heaven, but it could be. The *stuff* sometimes made it heaven. Today, heaven was the apartment buildings that lined the streets; these buildings were a uniform for Ridgewood: midsized rectangles six families or so high, green-painted iron fence lining the front stoop that protected the garbage pails and cellars, square windows that faced the street and fire escapes that led into unkempt alleyways, and each unit was adorned with a corbel millwork crown on top. Those crowns meant home. The neighborhood was postwar archi-tecture in some places, in others even older. Her mother told her of an old farmhouse that still stood near Cypress Avenue. Dezzy had never been there, but she figured if she wandered around enough, she'd find it. She could call it home.

"Home," she mumbled.

Dezzy reached her long, slender arm into her front jean pocket and searched the bottom. A smile spread across her face. It was still there. It was odd that it was still there, as Dezzy took care to throw most everything away. Not this thing. This slip of paper kept on hanging around. She knew why. It was something that Pauline, the Irish barmaid at Gorgeous George's Barbecue Bin and Bar, had given to her a few months back. Most of what she spoke became gospel and what she couldn't commit to memory she asked Pauline to pen on torn strips of loose leaf paper. Then she'd carry them around like quotes from the bible.

Home. This one was about home.

She slipped the paper between her two fingers and pulled it out of her pocket. It was quite crumpled and starting to fray, but the writing in blue ink could still be read clearly. She whispered it aloud.

"Home is where hell is."

It was just before dawn when Pauline had said it. The bar had officially closed hours before, but she'd let the regulars and high tippers stay a little later as long as they kept the roar to a minimum. The shutters were drawn, the front door locked, the lights softened. It was a time for a nightcap cocktail or two and a slow cleanup. Pauline took her time and hummed while straightening the stools and refilling the refrigerators with ice. The boys at the bar all offered to help and Pauline took them up on it, assigning them to the basement to bring up cases of this and that to restock the bar. It was then, while the boys were running up and down the stairs and she was wiping down the bar counter with a dirty-water-soaked dish towel, that Dezzy had heard it. It was spoken softly between the melody of a nighttime hum and the screech of barstools being dragged across the floor and back to their rightful position at the counter.

On another night, Pauline explained to Dezzy what she had meant.

"When I was a young girl back home—and my home was a little town right along the coast of Galway, mind you—I lived in a small house with my mother, father, and five brothers, and two sisters. The boys were all born first and were quite a few years older than us girls. It was rather strange growing up there. The close quarters made for some tense mornings in the bathroom. Oh, it was the worst. The boys would get up and get there while my sisters and I stood outside of the door pacing the narrow hallway that led from our bedrooms to the bathroom. Even that was tense because there really was no room to walk back and forth for one person, let alone two girls who had to use the bathroom. We would cry to Father, one after the other, but Father would shake his head and laugh before stomping down the stairs, screaming my mother's name. He would say that he had no time for crying daughters. It was breakfast time, and in our house, Father's breakfast came first. Then his sons, my brothers, they would eat next (once they would get their arses out of the bathroom). When the last of them made their way down the stairs to eat, my sisters and I wouldn't act like those five animals but would politely take turns using the toilet or what have you. We never spoke about why the boys treated us the way they did or why Father didn't help. It was just the way it was. By the time we made it down for breakfast, there was not much left and Mother was already asking us to scrub and clean the boy's plates. She had already taken care of my father and he was off for a day of work. I wasn't sure what Father did. Mother knew, but she only would tell us that he worked with his hands. Perhaps, come to think of it, she didn't know either. We did know he took the boys with him wherever he went and that they were all gone most of the day. Mother never said much while we were home; she always seemed battle-worn to me, like what she had seen or done during the past few years had led her to a silence in voice and in heart. One day I asked her if it was Father who had made her that way and she slapped me right across the mouth. That's when I knew it was Father that had done it to her. So I began to notice more, taking pains to pay closer attention when he came home. He was always stinking of some whiskey or some other booze, but that was always the way it was, ya know? I thought all fathers smelled that way. There was something more, though. It was the way he and my brothers cackled and laughed at my mother, together most of the time, even when she wasn't in the room. The house was so small she must have heard them. My sisters were too little to understand what was going on, but I listened and watched and knew. Mother was a prisoner and alone in a house that she kept for the men. My father, my brothers, even their friends and their brothers came and went in my house. My mother kept them all; she gave them food, she listened to their plans and their troubles, she let them laugh at her and spit at her from afar after they spent the day pretending to work. They weren't working. They were at the pub and I knew all about it. Mother must have known, too. But still she kept quiet. So there I was, a girl who knew the truth, who couldn't tell my mother I knew that truth and with young sisters who could never understand. Father kept with his ways, my brothers did too, but not me. I kept my anger and hate inside, but I did so while remembering it every day. I made a little saying up: Home is where hell is. I repeated it often, at all types of places! Even at church, after I'd go to confession, instead of saying Hail Marys sixteen times or so, there I'd be in the pew reciting 'home is where hell' is. I would no longer be deluded that home was a place I wanted to be, and I would not be silenced the way Mother was. I repeated that little mantra until I turned the age that made it okay to leave the place, and without saying goodbye or taking a personal possession, I found my way to the States. And here I am today. Yes, I am a barmaid, still serving some of the same men who treated their old ladies and daughters the same way back home, but I don't stay silent. I don't live in a hell or work in a hell. Hell is back in Galway with those boys who ran my life. I left that hell there. I am free. I am home now. And so, I still say those words, home is where hell is, now and again, just to remind myself of what not to accept. Usually nobody is listening. I am glad you were, though, Ms. Dezzy."

Dezzy didn't understand how it applied to her life at the time but knew that it was meant for her. She knew that it was her life Pauline was talking about.

Dezzy whispered again.

"Home is where hell is."

"What'd you say, darling?"

The voice startled her and she shook her head as she came out of the daydream. Upon first look, Dezzy was confused; the entire neighborhood had changed. She was now directly in front of Gorgeous George's Barbecue Bin. Across the street from that was Chicken Galore and her momma. Dezzy wondered how she made it all the way here as Pip had dropped her off almost a mile away. She likened it to driving and arriving at a destination and not remembering exactly what happened during the drive. She didn't remember making turns down blocks or passing houses, landmarks. She just arrived.

Dezzy laughed under her breath. The stuff must have kicked back in.

"Dezzy?"

It was the same voice again. She turned her face in the direction of where it was coming from and squinted. It was Kenny. He was standing in front of the Gorgeous George's dressed in a red t-shirt that read "Bass Master" in white across the chest.

"Oh. Hi, Ken."

He sipped on a beer and had the faint scent of the ocean about him. Dezzy smiled. She always liked Kenny. He took her fishing a few times and showed her how to bait the lines. He didn't do the *stuff*. She liked him even more.

"Jesus, kid, you better not let your mother see you like this."

"She's busy across the street working. She doesn't even know where I am. She never does."

He laughed. "She's looking out of the front glass door at you right now."

Dezzy turned. The dark of her momma's eyes were fixed right on hers. "Shit," she said. Momma's finger was pointed right at her and waving up and down. She couldn't hear her but watched as she mouthed Spanish curses at her from behind the closed glass door of Chicken Galore. It was hell.

Kenny laughed again. "I wish I could read lips; your mom is on fire right now."

Dezzy squirmed and turned back to Kenny. She had no intention of facing her mother right now. "Can we go inside, Ken?"

"Where? George's?"

"Anywhere."

"George is in there somewhere, just saying."

"I don't care."

"Let me finish my cigarette."

Dezzy turned around and looked at Momma again. Her yelling was fogging up the front door glass of Chicken Galore. The stuff began to wear off again. Dezzy grabbed Kenny's hand. "Can we just go in now?"

Kenny dragged on the butt and flicked it away. He looked over Dezzy's shoulder and waved at her mother, who was still standing at the door pointing. Dezzy's mother didn't wave back but put her hands on her hips. Kenny laughed again.

"Ken, please."

"Okay, let's go. I think Pauline might be the barmaid today." Kenny drained the beer and tossed it into the ashcan next to the no smoking sign. A sense of calm had returned to Dezzy's face.

"I know. I was just thinking about her."

"What did you say before? You said home is where hell is, right, hun?"

Dezzy smiled at Kenny again. He always knew what she said. He just liked to hear her say it again. She liked him.

Behind her, some of the front neon lights of Chicken Galore were burned out; they had been for a year or so. The sign only read "CHICK GAL" now. Momma hated the sign. She hated Chicken Galore. She even hated chicken. What she most hated now was Dezzy. The smile that came so easy to Dezzy moments before had reformed into a frown.

"I don't know what I said, Ken." She grabbed the door handle and noticed that the paper was still in her hand. Dezzy stuffed it back in her pocket. *Hell*, she thought. She had to face her momma sooner or later. That was later. Now, they both disappeared into the warm lights and scent of slowly roasting pork.

It was loud inside, but it always was loud in there. The place was built to be that way. Then there was Gorgeous George who was always decibels louder. The dining floor had no booths but was full of circle tables with four chairs each strewn across the large space. George wanted people to be able to drink and eat and talk openly; he often walked among them yelling and shouting. He took to it from the moment he came in until the lights went out. They called him Gorgeous George because he looked like the wrestler with the same name. The odd thing was he thought he looked more like Ric Flair, another wrestler who used to yell out "WOOOO!" to the crowd when he was in the ring. So that's just what George did. He'd walk around the bin and talk all kind of shit: how good his barbecue was, how good the drinks tasted, how much fun the people were going to have even before they were even having any fun.

Gorgeous George had the right idea, though; the place could be a lot of fun. It looked fun: red and orange Christmas lights streaked across the ceiling and through the bar—they always remained on. The floor was full of sawdust and peanut shells; it created the feel of a feathery carpet under shoe. Kenny spent most of his afternoons here. A gold-plated plaque on the back of one of the bar stools that read "Ken the Fisherman" had been presented to him on his tenth anniversary at the Bin. It was a special honor. None of the bar regulars got mad that Ken got his very own chair; they all loved him. They did, however, fight over who would get the next one. Gorgeous George had no intention of giving anyone else their own chair.

The yelling started from across dining hall. George was greeting a family who just walked in. He took to their young son right away and started working his act.

"WOOOOOO welcome to my Barbecue Bin, little man! You and your family find a nice seat and sit down—we have lots of goodies for you guys today. How about an adult drink for your dad? Mommy is going to drive, right? How about it, Dad? Oh, wait! Maybe Mommy needs that adult drink? WOOOOO! I say let's get you both one. Sit down and enjoy—WOOOOOOO!"

Kenny shook his head as he and Dezzy made their way to the bar. Sitting there ahead of them was Chris Graf. No one ever called him Chris Graf. He had been known as Tank since the sixth grade. Tank was a large man with large hands and a good heart. That good heart could turn bad and make those large hands do bad things on the wrong day. That day wasn't today. Tank was happier these days; he recently became a father to a little baby girl. The first time he held her, she barely fit in his hands. That's when he knew he had to get the bad out of those hands. It was his first child—and probably his last—but it didn't matter. Tank had his baby daughter. That's all he ever wanted.

"Have some suds and have a seat, hun." Tank stood up and gave Dezzy his chair. Another beer appeared at the bar and a boy with a beard handed it to her.

"I thought you said Pauline was the barmaid today, Ken?"

Kenny looked around as he drained another beer. "She was here, right, Tank?"

Tank nodded. "I think there might be two of them behind the bar today. She was in a bad mood or something, I don't know. It's pretty packed in here and, well, George said something to her and...." The yelling across the Bin started up again.

"WOOOOOOOO! We have ribs and smoked chicken butt today, Dad! Don't you want to wash that down with a sirloin steak? I know I do! WOOOOOO!"

Dezzy was peeling the label off of her beer. "Ken, how do you sit here day after day? George can be a real asshole."

Kenny laughed. "Nah, come on, the guy is hilarious. I have my own chair anyway. King of the castle!" He clanked his fresh beer against Tank's.

George heard the clank and raised his head.

"Hey Kenny! WOOOOOO! There you are!" George came toward them lightning fast. He tapped the back of the chairs of some of the people sitting and eating at their tables as he passed by. No one looked up or even reacted to this; it was as if they had come to accept everything that George was going to do to them during their meals: the screaming, the barking, and the bullshit. The trade-off was the best dirt-cheap barbecue for miles. George knew it. They all knew it. Forks stabbed the pork and George WOO'd from dawn to dusk. The worm kept on turning.

Dezzy pulled her face into her shirt in an attempt to hide. It was no use. There were two hells to choose from today. Some days there were different hells, more than two, sometimes three or four. Today it was Momma across the street or Gorgeous George in the bin. George, with his wavy white hair and spray-on tan, was torpedoing toward them. Behind the entrance door and across the street were Momma and her angry eyes. Dezzy could somehow now feel the piece of paper with the writing on it in her pocket. It was no use to move. She picked up the beer and took a huge hit. For now, she would stay the course.

It started.

"WOOO! Look at this little crowd! The three of ya! Kenny, give me a hug, baby. When did you get here?"

"About noon."

"Beautiful! Have another beer! Tank, what about you? And you are looking good by the way, Mister New Daddy. Congratulations!"

"Thanks man, she's my world."

"WOOOO! I just can't wait to get your little missy in here for a little barbecue."

Kenny slapped George on the arm. "She doesn't have any teeth, you idiot. How is she gonna eat barbecue?"

"Baby food barbecue then! WOOOO!" yelled George. Tank didn't laugh. That wasn't his usual way. Most times he laughed at anything George, Kenny, just about anyone, said. Something had changed in him when he found out his wife was pregnant, he was going to be a father, and that the baby was to be a little girl. It was then he didn't care much to be Tank anymore. While driving his route in the delivery truck, he often thought of the little baby wrapped in a pink and white, soft, knit blanket his grandmother had given to her on the day she was born. There the baby would lie, softly sleeping, unaware he was working double-time to make sure the house stayed warm and the electric stayed on. Every morning he'd set his alarm an hour early so he could get up before he had to leave for work just to sit and hold her tiny new hand in the dark. Hers wouldn't be a childhood that he had inherited from a drunken mother and a dishonest father. Hers wouldn't be screaming and shoving on the stoop at midnight. He would move away from Cypress Avenue and leave the gum tar and the street sweepers stuck to the sidewalk and gutters. He didn't need to be a tank anymore. He didn't want to be a tank anymore. He was now Chris again. He was a daddy to his daughter. Chris didn't much like talking about his daughter. Not in this place, and never with a son of a bitch like George.

Chris wasn't a son of a bitch however. He smiled and took a sip of his beer.

"Maybe I'll bring her in soon. Once things settle down and she gets a little bigger."

"And she grows some teeth." Kenny and Tank clanked their beers again and got up to go for a smoke. George waved his hands at them in disgust as he turned to Dezzy.

"And what about you, Dezzy? No Sam Jean looking up your skirt today?"

Dezzy fingered the piece of paper in her pocket again.

"No? Nothing going up there these days? You gonna let me up there one day?"

There was no answer. George leaned in. His neck was oiled with Stetson cologne. It burned Dezzy's eyes.

"I bet that old bastard is screwing you six ways to Sunday."

Her thoughts turned to Sam Jean. He would need his evening wine soon. The only thing getting screwed in the apartment was the cork. George could never understand that. There was no reason to even explain it to him. Dezzy spent the days watering Sam's plants and folding the laundry before the two of them could listen to talk radio on the couch until he fell asleep. It was more a home to her than she had ever known and that's all it would ever be. Most men could never accept that. Dezzy remembered Pauline and her father and brothers. She even thought of her own goddamn father. The paper made sense now. Men use and use their women until there is nothing left but a half-beating heart and a hell to call home.

She wanted out of the Bin. George brought her back in.

"I know you can hear me, baby. I just want to know how you taste."

Then it happened. It happened fast. From out of nowhere, Pauline appeared, walked up to George, and punched him squarely in the jaw. He dropped, hit his head on the bar, and fell straight to the ground. The impact on the bar had injured his head and blood was everywhere. Pauline spit on him as he rolled underneath Kenny's personalized chair, moaning in pain.

"George, you son of a bitch, I quit. And leave this young girl alone. Dezzy, you go home now." Dezzy was stunned at everything that just transpired but nodded.

Pauline walked out of the front door and left George groaning on the floor among the sawdust and peanut shells. The Bin was silent.

The front door whipped back open.

"Holy shit, what happened in here?" Kenny and Tank rushed over and crowded around George. His long white hair was full of dark red blood.

"What the hell? Oh man, he's hurt! Someone call an ambulance! Dezzy, what happened?"

Dezzy didn't answer Kenny. Soon enough they all would figure it out. George would be okay, this wasn't the first time he had been punched in the face by a woman, and it wouldn't be the last. *Men like this don't learn from these things or get what is coming to them like this*, Dezzy thought. George knew it. It came with being a son of a bitch.

She grabbed her beer and walked out into the fading afternoon. Nobody stopped her. It was time for Sam Jean's wine. It was time for home.

An alarm or radar must have gone off because as soon as she pushed through the front door, there was Momma standing across the street in front of Chicken Galore, waiting for her. The beer slipped from Dezzy's hands and shattered. Brown shards exploded in every direction.

"Oh my God."

Momma had chicken fat and blood on her face and a spatula full of chicken grease in her hand. Dezzy froze. Momma started yelling and waving her hands at her daughter. The spatula sent the chicken grease up in the air and back down on Momma's hair. This made her even angrier.

"Desponda! There you are! Get your ass over here now! Where have you been? Hanging around with that drug dealer? Or were you with that old man? Desponda, get over here! Ay, the chicken grease is everywhere!"

Her shouts were echoing off the apartment buildings. A woman on the third floor of her building had opened her window and hung out of it to see what was going on. The more Momma yelled, the more Dezzy noticed people stopping, staring, whispering. It seemed as if the entire avenue had turned in her direction. There was nothing Dezzy could do. Momma didn't notice, she just yelled louder.

"You see what you make me do? I have to work and worry about you all day long! You going with this guy and that one and hanging out in bars! I can't live like this! You get home now, Desponda!"

Tears filled Dezzy's eyes now. "Momma, I can't, I got to go. Momma. I'm sorry."

"You're gonna be sorry! I'm going to hand your ass to you if you don't get over here right now! Desponda, *ahora aqui*!!" Momma tried to throw the spatula across the avenue at Dezzy. It hit an oncoming car and disappeared.

"No, Momma, NO!" and Dezzy took off running as fast as she could away from everything: Momma, the Barbecue Bin, Kenny, Tank and his newborn daughter, Gorgeous George, Pip's car, the stuff, even the worm turning. Dezzy knew there was no way to stop any of it. She ran harder. More people on the street stood and watched the action of that old woman in a blue shirt with a dancing chicken on it racing down the sidewalk, yelling and waving her hands in the air wildly after her daughter.

Dezzy slid her hand across the iron pointed tops of the front gate fences as she raced by them. Hell; this was her hell: Cypress Avenue and all of its shit. The urge never came to look back.

Momma had already stopped running; her voice and chicken grease faded into the green graffiti-coated mailboxes and defunct Johnny pumps of Cypress Avenue. It didn't matter to Dezzy. She was running all the way back to Sam Jean's apartment. There was wine to be poured and hells to be left behind.

PART 2

Salvation on himrod Street

It was hot. Betty had already turned on both the overhead and the oscillating fan on their highest settings. The sultry air brushed her hair over her ears but didn't do much by the way of comfort. The afternoon sun was strong now; it filtered through the window, filling the entirety of the kitchen. Betty didn't believe in curtains or drapes. Five clear glass windows were built into the apartment: two facing the street, one by the air chute, and two above the unkempt patio yard. Betty washed that glass clean every other day. Today was the other day, but it was far too hot for cleaning. It didn't matter too much. The remaining raindrops that stuck on the glass fractured the light, turning it into what looked like sparkling white tears. Betty looked forward to seeing them. The shadows of those light tears dotted the yellow wallpaper that was fitted throughout the kitchen and in the living room. Betty liked living in those shadows. The rain came often to Himrod Street and so followed the raindrop shadows.

The yellow wallpaper still looked nice, she thought. She and Benjamin Zogby put it up together all in one weekend, on a summer afternoon a lot like this one, many years ago. The apartment belonged to Betty's great-aunt, but she let them stay in the middle room for only twenty dollars per week. Some of their friends thought they were crazy; it was already bright in the apartment and adding the yellow wallpaper would just about make it blinding. Betty's great-aunt was half-blind and didn't care. Betty and Zogby didn't care. They chose it then because it was bright and warm, very much as they were at that time. They loved sunlight. They loved the beach. During the time the yellow wallpaper went up, they lived between the raindrops.

"Betty, what are you staring at?"

Betty was pouring a cup of tea for Father White. He sat with his legs crossed at the small, white kitchen table. The daydream came to an abrupt stop.

"Nothing, just the wallpaper."

Father White surveyed it for himself. "It's charming. It seems as if the floral pattern is fading in some places, but overall I'd say it looks very nice. Did it come with the apartment?"

The tea steeped as it filled the small, floral-patterned teacups. Betty turned her back and went to the cabinet for two saucers.

"Ben and I put it up when we moved in."

"The Corporal?"

Betty stood silent. She reached and ran her fingertips across the yellow wallpaper. It still felt new.

"Funny you should mention him; he's part of the reason I came to visit you today."

Betty set the tea on the table and returned to the fridge. She threw the quart of milk on the table, barely missing Father White's teacup. "I wish you wouldn't have told me that."

"There's no need to do that now. I wasn't trying to be unpleasant to you."

"What were you trying to do, then?"

"Not be unpleasant."

Betty laughed.

"It was you that just brought his name up; I happened to see him this morning and so I mentioned it, that's all," he persisted.

"Right, that's *all*."

"That's right. I'm going to roll a cigarette, do you want one?"

"Yes."

Betty sat down across from Father White while he worked the bag of tobacco and the rolling papers. The process was one that she had seen many times, and always at the kitchen table. Perhaps the kitchen table had some sort of meaning. They always ended up there; never to eat but to wade through the uncomfortable reason they were there in the first place. She did not make eye contact with him while pouring the sugar in her cup, but he kept his eyes on her, never looking down, as he rolled the cigarettes. The raindrop shadows began to fade as the sunlight burned them away.

Father John looked around the kitchen.

"So, you thinking of changing the paper in here?"

The spoon clanked loudly as she stirred the tea while Father White licked the rolling paper, sealing it closed with a flick of his lighter. The raindrop shadows were just about gone.

"It's such a shade of yellow now, Betty. Ain't possible it always was this ugly color, is it?"

Silence.

Betty reached over and grabbed the cigarette out of his hands and tapped the end of it on the table to settle the tobacco. The steady tapping grew louder.

"Would you like to use my lighter?" asked Father John. Betty raised her eyebrows in agreement. He offered it to her and she grabbed it quickly, flicking on a flame in his face before lighting up the cigarette. A huge cloud of smoke settled overhead and hung there like a storm cloud.

"Just like him," Father John mumbled.

"I like the ugly wallpaper, if you must know. I have no intentions of ever changing it."

"Is that right?"

Betty nodded her head yes and blew another puff of smoke into the air. The air in the room grew denser now; the heat of the day was thickening, the smoke making it so it could stick to everything around them. Father John began to roll another cigarette. He reached for the tea and took a sip.

"This is some lovely tea you have made, by the way."

Betty raised her eyebrows. "It's Lipton."

"Is it? Well, you brewed Mister Lipton perfectly. I hear it's good to drink something hot on a warm day because it forces your body to cool off."

Betty stood up and flicked her ash in the sink. "You almost done?"

"Almost, thank you. Wasn't there a short story written by a feminist writer called 'The Yellow Wallpaper'? I can recall my sister writing an essay about it when she was a little girl in grade school."

Betty scratched her ass and shrugged her shoulders as she picked up her teacup. Father John frowned.

"Well, I thought that perhaps you and the Corporal decorated with this here color paper because of that story. I always thought you a well-read woman, Betty."

"Well, I don't know that one."

"You should. This apartment is very much like the home in that story; lots of sunlight and windows and yellow."

"I wouldn't know."

Father John felt the duel coming.

"I can probably get you a copy."

"That's not necessary."

"Oh, but you'd really take something away from it. See, the lady in the story is locked in this room with yellow wallpaper. Very much like this. She eventually strips off the yellow wallpaper, freeing her body from a self-imposed prison."

Betty dragged on her cigarette and tapped her foot impatiently.

"The husband is the key to it all."

"I don't care."

"See, the husband gave her that room to stay in while he went off and did this and that. She eventually found salvation in the yellow wallpaper being removed."

"Stop it, Father."

"Barnes and Nobles has a copy; we can have tea and read it."

"No, we can't."

"I'll call Zogby; we can read it together."

"Don't you bring his name up to me!"

Betty launched the teacup at the wall and it exploded above Father John's head, sending the fake porcelain pieces across the kitchen. The tea was everywhere; what tea hadn't seeped into Father John's jacket pooled on the floor underneath the kitchen table, soaking his shoes straight through to the socks. It felt like cold rain.

She stood up and paced around the kitchen as she yelled. "Well-read woman, my ass! Yellow wallpaper! Give me a goddamn break, Father. Why don't you just clear out of here? You got what you came for, there's no need to talk. You don't give a shit about anything here."

A banging came through the wall from across the hallway.

"Is everything all right in there?" a voice shouted.

Betty shouted back. "Yes, sorry, Ms. Madre! I slipped and a glass broke. I am fine."

Father John put down his cup and picked out some of the thin white broken pieces of Betty's cup that were floating on top of the still-steaming liquid. He sprinkled them on the floor under his shoe and rubbed them into the linoleum and spilt tea. They crackled and crunched with each turn under his foot. He kept his eyes on Betty until the crunching stopped. The chair across from Father White screeched across the floor as Betty made room to sit down in it.

"John…why do you bring him up to me? I don't want to talk to you about him. We have this, whatever this is—our arrangement. You got what you came for. Why must you bring him up to me?"

"You brought him up."

"Oh, goddamn you. You know exactly what I mean."

Father John went to light his cigarette. It was moist with tea. He tossed it on the table in disgust. "Perhaps I have been wondering why someone would make such an arrangement like this."

She didn't answer.

Betty knew exactly why she made the arrangement. It all started after she had moved back to the neighborhood five years ago. There was a huge risk in moving back here, as the neighborhood was a virtual Mobius loop; it never changed and the people never changed; one could use the Ridgewood phone book to connect the dots of names and phone numbers to their corresponding hookups and street fights. There was always some idiot on a stoop with nothing to do but talk to another idiot on their stoop next door about who was moving in or out. Moving back in would be a bit of chess and take a bit of luck. Her new apartment had once belonged to her great-aunt. After she passed, the landlord granted her late great-aunt's wish for her to take it over as long as he could raise the rent a few bucks. There was always a condition when it came to people. The money wasn't a problem; it would buy her a place that was far enough away from Cypress Avenue and most of the people she knew.

Once settled in, she found that those that had mattered most were either long dead or had moved away. The thought of it put her at ease, but she knew there were still plenty of eyes that she had to avoid; facing Zogby would never be an option—not for her. For the first few months, she kept to herself, leaving the house only to run to the local grocery store or to get her hair cut. Both places were on the same block. It didn't bother her much because it was winter-time and the city had been caught in a deep cold spell. She watched the world from her window as the temperature barely rose above twenty degrees and the wind was blowing all the time.

By early spring, she grew more confident, venturing deeper into Ridgewood, even walking down the full length of Cypress Avenue one afternoon. It was that day when she passed by St. Aloysius. The pull to walk through the doors proved to be too much; she had wanted to light a prayer candle for her great-aunt since her first day in the apartment. No one would notice.

There in the shadows and electric orange candlelight is where she met Father John. He knelt down next to her and asked if he could pray for whoever it was she was praying for. She didn't remember his face and he seemed not to recognize hers, so she went along with it. After finishing their prayers, they quietly spoke. His voice was soft and credulous; it didn't take long for her to think his suggestion that they go to the confessional was a good one. The dark made it easy for her to talk about everything, especially Benjamin Zogby. There wasn't much she left out about her time on Cypress Avenue.

After she had finished, Father White came into her side of the confessional and locked the door. He told her there was some confessing he had to do as well. Fear and horror came over her when he revealed that he lived upstairs from

Benjamin Zogby, that the two were friends, and that he had confided many things in him about her; in the confessional and in the apartment, even on the stoop. He repeated all the things Zogby had said she had done to him and explained to her the shell of the man that he had become because of those things. She wept through it all. When she was done crying, she heard herself agree to Father John's second suggestion of coming over later to discuss what to do about it.

That night, through ancient tears and bad wine, they went to bed. He promised her he would never reveal to anyone, especially Zogby, that she had returned. There was a condition. There is always a condition when dealing with people. He asked only that he could visit her now and again so they could pray together and that one day; she could give herself and Zogby peace through the Lord. Through more tears she agreed.

Now and again turned into every week, prayers turned into perversion, and regret into resentment. She barely left the apartment anymore. It was done. This whole agreement assured that she never had to face Benjamin Zogby again. Father John White had kept his holy promise. It was then she knew the pact she had made had been with the devil.

Betty and Father John were still at the table. They were both silent. The second floor neighbors held their ears steadfast to their apartment doors, listening. It was a few minutes before Father John spoke

"Okay, Betty. I better get going. There's a lot to do…at the church today, anyways. You stay blessed."

He pushed back the chair and stood up while removing his hat. He shook off the shards that had fallen into the brim and took the remainder of his tea down in one gulp, closed the apartment door behind him, and walked down the staircase.

At the bottom of the landing stood a girl. Father John recognized her right away. It was Sarah Jane. She was fifty years younger than Betty and full of soft features that needed hardening. *What life and bad luck wouldn't do was to be left to the wolves*, he thought.

She was early for their regular meeting. That was normal. She also must have followed him here. Usually that would alarm him a bit, but it didn't matter much. As long as she had gin and some cocktail jazz back at her place he would go along.

Father John crouched down on the bottom step, his face at her belt buckle. Sarah Jane didn't look at him when she spoke.

"Father, why are you still here?"

"Do you not want me to be?"

"I don't know."

"What don't you know?"

"Maybe I shouldn't say."

"No, you should say it. Maybe I could help you. What don't you know?"

"If what we are doing is right."

"Oh. Well, of course it isn't."

"So, we should stop?"

"Absolutely."

Sarah took a step back.

"Father, I don't want to stop."

"I know. I don't either."

"But it isn't right. You're a...."

"I'm what?"

Sarah Jane paused and looked away.

"I'm thinking."

"What could you be thinking about right now except my hand on your thigh and what kind of drink you're going to make me when we get to your apartment?"

"Not that and not that."

"Then what?"

Sarah Jane's voice became a whisper. She pulled his face close to hers.

"Father John, do you believe in the devil?"

"Who? The devil?"

"Yes."

"You're thinking about the devil?"

"Or Lucifer."

Father John stood up. His throat was parched from the heat and cigarette smoke in Betty's apartment. The gin would be cold at Sarah Jane's apartment. He started to work out of the conversation.

"The devil and Lucifer are two different things. I don't confuse the two a t'all."

"How do you know?"

"Well, it's a fact and is written in the earliest parts of the Holy Bible. Lucifer or Satan is the snake. You know the one I am referring to don'cha? The one snake that tempted Adam and Eve in that there Garden of Eden. You know that story?"

"I don't read the Bible often Father."

"You don't need to. I am a walking bible, Miss Sarah Jane. The devil, now, he is different, see? He is that which influences mankind, oh, and womankind, in the heart. You know what they say, right? A person can be full of devils. They never say a person can be full of Lucifers, right?

"I don't know. I don't pay attention to most people."

"Well then, there you go. Now you know. Come on, let's go."

"Okay."

"You sure?"

"No."

"Well, spit it out then."

"Okay...I saw Lucifer once. Well, I guess after what you just said, I saw the devil."

"Oh, come on."

"I did, Father. I swear I really did."

Father John stood up. This is not the Sunday afternoon he had hoped for. He grabbed Sarah Jane on the shoulders and shook her a bit. He had enough of it all.

"Sarah, don't you think this all sounds a little nutty? Where you reckon you saw him?"

"Very close to Cypress Avenue, Father."

"Oh, did you? Was he red-skinned top to bottom with hoofs and tail, too?"

"Not exactly."

"No? Was he living in Highland Park in a tent or something? Maybe it was someone in a Halloween costume."

"I don't think so, Father. I did see him though. I swear it."

Father John let her go and walked passed her to the front door.

"I'm just telling you so you know, Father. See, I've been thinking. Now hear me out, please, before we go. Maybe what we are doing here, you and I, is because of the devil or Lucifer or whatever—some kind of evil. Maybe everything that has been happening around Cypress Avenue has to do with the devil."

"The devil…."

"Yes. I am going to say this because I have to. I truly sincerely saw the devil and when he looked at me I knew, all that we've been doing is evil. You are a priest, I am…. This is just all wrong. And now here we are adding to the dirt and smut already caked up on the people of Cypress Avenue. I came to you after I saw him because I thought you knew the way out, but no, he found his way to you too, didn't he? He brought us together in this. I had to just see it through, Father. You know that now, don't you? I know the devil exists. He is here on Cypress Avenue."

Sarah Jane began crying in the hallway. The tenant on the bottom floor opened his door and peered out from behind the still-attached chain lock. When Father John noticed him, the door quickly shut and the lock turned.

A cell phone ring went off, cutting through Sarah Jane's crying. It was Father John White's phone. The number wasn't familiar. He let it ring twice before answering.

"Hello? Yes? Okay. Yes I am. Who? I see. My God. Are you sure? Okay. I will be right there."

Sarah Jane stopped crying.

"Who was that, Father?"

There was a long pause and deep sigh. Father John looked up to Betty's apartment. The hallway was dark there, it always was dark there. It would get darker now, no matter how yellow the wallpaper.

He walked back to Sarah Jane and knelt beside her.

"You might have been right, Sarah Jane. Now I want you to listen closely; I want you to sit here and pray and say none of what happened here, to anybody. And nothing about *you-know-who that you saw* to anyone, okay? I am sure it will just make it all worse."

"Okay."

"Do you understand?"

"I think so."

"I have to go now."

"I know."

"Just don't tell anyone, okay? Not your mommy or your daddy or anyone. Let us with the church deal with all of it."

"Okay, Father. I swear I won't."

"There is one thing I want you to do, though."

Sarah Jane nodded.

Father John pulled a piece of paper from his pocket notepad and stared hard at it. It took a few moments, but he scribbled a note between the light blue lines and folded it into a small square. He handed it to Sarah Jane.

"Now there is a woman up on two; she is the second door in, 2B. Her name is Betty. I want you to go up there after saying fifty Hail Marys and fifty Our Fathers, knock on her door, and hand her this paper. Sarah, do make sure you hand her this paper. Tell her it's from me. Don't stand there after you hand it to her. Turn and run back down the stairs and out the front door. Don't stop until you get home. I will meet you there."

Sarah Jane nodded.

"And don't worry about the devil. Think of salvation, Sarah Jane. Be salvation."

It was all over as soon as the door closed and its locks realigned. Father John was gone. Sarah Jane stayed in place and prepared to pray but all she could think of was the devil and the time she saw him in her apartment on Himrod Street:

She recalled a dim haze of cigarette smoke swirling over the headboard of her bed. She watched it snake and slip across the back wall before evaporating through the half-open window. A ghost, that's what it was. A phantasm of the heart, she thought. The ghost sat on the bed next to her and blew another puff of smoke into the air. She remembered taking the cigarette out of the ghost's hand and putting it in her mouth. She hated smoking. She pulled and exhaled. The smoke didn't have the same effect as before. Perhaps it was evil, the fire and brimstone kind. She saw it as elusive Lucifer. There was a star of the same name that hung in the winter evening sky. Her parents told of it often, right before her bedtime stories. So did the ghost. He whispered in her ear about an everlasting light that was greater than any light that had shone in the night sky before. Its light was only available to those who truly looked for it. She and her inherited green eyes looked for it more than any other star. Her view from Himrod Street was obscured by the city light that came from midtown Manhattan, and then as the years went on, Manhattan the lower, and finally the entire tri-state. It bathed the heavens in plastic. She longed for the chance to live among flat open spaces and no cities. She longed to see the Lucifer star. The ghost told her he knew the way how. Then she got scared. It wasn't a star or Lucifer, it was the devil.

That was on Friday.

It was now Sunday and the devil was on Cypress Avenue. Just outside the double-sided, black-painted steel door.

On the other side of that door sat Sarah Jane. She followed Father John's instructions and began to pray on the bottom step of the staircase landing among the roaches and fire retardant.

back at Nunny's

The truck had taken a little more than several hours to unload, but it was finally unloaded and the boxes were packed away in the basement. Dave and Keith stood in the doorway of Nunny's and watched the delivery truck pull away. The delivery was ordered to be six hundred pieces, but an extra seventy-five cases of product came along with it. Someone screwed up. The deliveryman wasn't at fault but he would be blamed, and had he returned with the wrong stuff, his paycheck would be taxed. Not the supervisor, or his supervisor, or the general manager would lose a dime in their take-home pay; it would be the deliveryman. It seemed that the ways of the world these days seeped down to every level of life. Keith hated that most. The deliveryman explained that he was already living check-to-check and he begged them to take the extra pieces. There was no hesitation. A two-hour job had transformed into a four-hour grinder; the back-and-forth had taken a lot out of them, even with the delivery guy helping in the basement.

Now it was over; the deliveryman was a little buzzed on champagne and driving his truck back to the plant. As he honked the horn to say goodbye to the boys, all he could think of was beating the traffic, parking the truck in the lot, punching his time card out, collecting his pay, crossing the street, and sitting on the edge of a stool at Cranberries Irish Pub until closing time.

Dave waved after the last blast of the truck horn echoed across the avenue and turned to Keith.

"That truck was a son of a bitch."

"It always is."

"My legs are shot, man."

"It's the heat; it zaps the life out of you."

"It's not the heat, it's the truck. It's trying to kill me. That goddamn truck is trying to kill me."

"Kill *us* Dave. And it always will."

They stood there with their hands on their hips, breathing hard. The truck never got easier. In this, their twenty-fifth year at Nunny's, delivery day was still the most dreaded part of the week. It never failed to come, either, and for years the truck had come on a Wednesday morning. Last month it changed. One day Keith got a call from the distribution company saying they would now ship their orders every Sunday afternoon. The management there never explained fully why the change in delivery day; they just said it was the new business model. That wasn't the reason. Keith figured out they most likely had an ethnic variety of undocumented Latino and Mexican help working for a few dollars at the warehouse loading the trucks. Doing this business on a Sunday was the model and with good reason; most of those who kept an eye on this type of stuff either looked the other way or had their eyes glued to the game on television. The watchdogs in America didn't have time for ethics and righteousness on a Sunday. It was an off day. They'd be back at it Monday.

Meanwhile, Keith and Dave clung to life on a Sunday.

Dave ran his fingers through his hair and shook the sweat out. He and Keith stared at each other.

"Now that we have a second here, what the hell was all of that stuff that went on earlier?"

Keith looked around. Cypress Avenue was its usual Sunday quiet. He still wanted to go inside.

"I don't know exactly, but let's go inside before we talk about any of it." The door latch released and the store door closed behind them.

Keith grabbed a fresh bottle of champagne and turned the radio to the classic rock station. The song that came over the radio was something from Pearl Jam. Dave poured himself a cup and did a drumroll on the countertop before he spun the radio dial away from Pearl Jam.

"I like this song, but this isn't classic rock; it's nineties rock."

Keith was nodding in agreement as the cork came loose and popped into his hand.

"They call the station classic rock and then only play *Stairway to Heaven* and *Dream On* by Aerosmith seventy times a day. The rest of the programming is Pearl Jam. Radio is garbage, my friend."

Dave had felt the same way for years. He continued after a sip of bubbles. "You're right and I can't stand it, goddammit. Look how mechanically generated and neatly packaged the music present on MTV and VH1's airwaves has become.

Look at the radio! How easily have these radio stations with any contemporary format have readily turned to *American Idol* winners, the sloppy seconds of grunge and metal and the bluesy rock days of the late sixties and throughout the seventies. I don't know where the wheel spun the wrong way; maybe it was all the fault of free downloads hosted by Napster. Perhaps greedy record producers and owners were pressuring their programmers and musicians to produce the same soft visceral crap that leaves my mother…."

"Who is an accomplished singer and musician but has since rolled over to the happy endings of fairy tales and pop music," mumbled Keith.

"That's right. She's so numb to it that she is left tapping her right foot like she is Sammy Davis Jr. on crack. There is a slew of these new groups masquerading as music that have crapped it all up for those of us with a decent set of ears placed alongside our temples, and some of us have them set on top of our head like the dogs we were meant to be."

Keith drained his cup and poured another.

Dave was just getting started. "It's a combination of yesterday's and today's sound mixed all together to create this mutant of corporate music because no one is really sure how to give us something completely fresh and new; especially not those in charge of the radio stations."

The guitar solo of the Pearl Jam song continued on and on.

"Let's stay away from the idea of Nirvana and Soundgarden, shit, even Pearl Jam being the answer in 1991, and look to what came after the Seattle scene: a swell of good, and then nothing. There was a lot of great hip-hop, rock, electronica, indie, and rhythm-and-blues acts that emerged; some even still co-exist with the hybrid manufactured versions of music today, but none made a scene to stand on. And the radio stations lap this crap up."

"I'm going to lap up this drink."

Dave stopped and sighed. Keith tried not to laugh by keeping the cup close to his mouth; he had heard this whole thing before and couldn't help but interrupt Dave's diatribe.

"No, seriously. There has been nothing that coaxed the sleep out of the sixties à la Beatles, and nothing that filled the summer air of '71 through 1980—which, of course, culminated with John Lennon's death—like the Led Zeppelin. The '80s were transgendered years of metal and makeup—to the extreme. Remember garbage bands like Warrant and Dokken and Poison with that album *Look What the Cat Dragged In*? Nothing was truer than the arm-pumping, anarchy finger spread that was an arena full of metal kids! That's what I miss: the passion and real musicians. What has the last seven years brought us in the way of music? For me it has been a steady diet of every act or group or band or rapper I have listened to before with an occasional sprinkling of a new face with some razzle-dazzle here and there. Mostly I keep with contemporary music because I don't want to be an old miser at a party full of know-nothings."

Dave tuned the radio back to the classic rock station. Pearl Jam ended. The radio ID played over some obnoxious buzzing sound effects and Aerosmith's "What It Takes" cycled through next.

Keith poured champagne and shrugged his shoulders. "You can't make this stuff up. Look at that. What about you, Goldie?"

"Screw radio!" Goldie was slumped in the chair behind the counter. She pointed her one free hand to the sky and drained the rest of her champagne with the other. Immediately after it was all gone, she stuck out her cup for more. Dave shrugged and gave her another splash.

Goldie didn't care much for the champagne but she couldn't complain either; her morning and afternoon so far consisted of refilling her cup full of bubbles, taking it all down in one shot, and refilling the thing again.

Dave did another drumroll on the countertop and one of Mario's honey-dripped sprinkle cookies fell off the plate and disappeared under the ping-pong table. None of the customers had eaten any cookies and they were beginning to melt. Usually the air conditioner would prevent this, even on a delivery day, but with the extra pieces of inventory the front door was open longer than it could handle. Dave reached down, picked up the cookie, and deposited it into the trash. Keith followed him with the rest of cookie plate.

"Man, that whole thing with Tina and then Mario today. All was going so great and then bam. It all went wrong." Dave wondered if they imagined it all.

CHING CHING

Everyone looked up. It was Father John White. The sunlight poured in behind him, bathing his body in a bright white-and-yellow glow. The sight of him made Goldie immediately think of the archangel Michael, the Lord's avenger. As he walked towards him, the sun was partially obscured by a cloud cutting off the light around him. Goldie then remembered Father John was more of a drunk than an angel. His arrival always heralded some news; could be small neighborhood gossip or even something that might affect the day-to-day of everyone for the next three months. The radio was lowered and another glass of champagne was poured. Goldie stood up and saluted.

"I am ready for my confession. Bless me for I have sinned over a thousand times this last week. My last confession was last week."

Father John ignored Goldie and refused the champagne. The sun was again free from behind the cloud and continued to burn the storefront of Nunny's. The heat was unforgiving; sweat began pouring down his face from beneath his hat, stinging his eyes. The only relief he could find was when he dotted his forehead with his pocket handkerchief. The heat ignited the scent of Old Spice and cigarettes, spreading it across store.

"Thank you, Keith, but I think bourbon would do me better right now."

A bottle of Jim Beam stood half open next to the radio. Keith grabbed a fresh cup from behind the bar.

"Save the cup, Keith. Hand me the bottle."

Keith put the cup back and stared at Dave. "What's going on, John?"

"Just please give me the bottle."

"Okay, but we've had enough shit in here today. Can you just get on with it?"

"Fair enough. I will. After you hand me that bottle."

Keith brought the bottle to the countertop and placed it in front of Father John. The look of it stirred up a smell in the preacher's nose. He hated whiskey. Whiskey interfered with everything: sex, sleep, homilies. This time it was fuel for the bearer of bad news. The brown liquid shook in the glass as he removed the cap and took a swig off the top. The volume on the radio was very low but they heard the station give its ID and the time.

It was 3:00 p.m.

Goldie sat up straight and didn't drink before the preacher spoke.

"Our friend Benjamin Zogby has been called home by the Lord."

No one said a word, but shook their heads before taking a drink. The sunlight began to fade as a massive grey-and-white cloud reappeared over the sun, this time blocking out its rays completely. A cold gray descended across the length of Cypress Avenue and filtered into Nunny's.

"Was it his heart?" asked Goldie.

Father John took another swig of the bourbon. "Not exactly."

"Who found him? You?"

"No, the police called me."

Keith refilled Dave and Goldie's cup. "Well, Father, whatever happened; I just hope that it happened quickly."

"That it did, Keith."

The cloud persisted over the sun, keeping the store and the avenue in a strange dark. There always seemed to be a strange dark on Cypress Avenue; Goldie could only describe it as a late-afternoon, gray-winter hue that hung over the day. It had been that way for years, and for years she and the rest of the residents of Cypress Avenue accepted the dark. Through drink and assorted powders, they accepted it. Through screeches and shrieks, they accepted it. The days blended into the evenings without providing answers. Ben Zogby on his stoop, Keith and Dave in the liquor store, Father John privately preaching to young girls in the dark, Tina telling murder stories about Earl, and Mario with his cookies and his cane hovering like impending doom over the avenue. There was no reason for any of it. Goldie was tired of accepting the dark. Today she needed an answer. She stood up and grabbed Father John's hand.

"What exactly happened to him, John?"

"Betty happened to him."

"What did Betty do John?"

"She finished off what she had been doing to him for years."

"What did she finish? What do you mean?"

Father John grabbed the bourbon and unscrewed the top. Before he could take a third swig, Goldie lunged at him, knocking the bottle off the counter and spilling what was left of the bourbon across the floor. She let go of his arm and screamed in his face.

"Tell me what happened to him, John!"

Crepuscular rays broke through the giant cloud, made their way to the entrance of Nunny's, and spread to the ground, scattering the gray. It was Jacob's Ladder. Father John adjusted his tie and looked up at Goldie.

"He shot himself on his stoop this afternoon in front of his niece and her friend."

Through a strange silence Father John bent over and picked up the empty bottle of bourbon, screwed the cap back on, and cradled it in his arms like a baby.

"I sure do hate whiskey...but I think it best we open another bottle, boys."

Dave nodded.

au Point Mort

dezzy grabbed the old green terrycloth and slowly dried the freshly-washed dishes; she had seen the suds pass over this particular set many times before. It seemed as if Sam always ate off the same five plates. They were very old, older than he was, and their pattern was familiar: blue-and-white ceramic majolica oyster plates that Sam brought home after a trip to France. Dezzy never ate off the plates. Her time with the plates was spent washing, drying, and returning them back to the cabinets over the sink. What the dish towel didn't take care of would be finished off by the heat, she thought. The work was almost done and there was a fresh bottle of wine in the refrigerator. The floor needed some sweeping, but besides that, the apartment was just as she had left it that morning. It always was. The apartment didn't see much movement; Sam had everything arranged the way it was going to be until he was carted out of the place by paramedics or the devil. He told that to Dezzy once. She wrote it down on a piece of torn loose-leaf and stuffed it in her jeans' front pocket. Sam's words lived in the opposite pocket of Pauline's and Dezzy kept them there ready, like she was a gunslinger and they were her guns to use when she needed them.

The last plate was dried and packed in the drainboard. Dezzy dragged the dish towel across the sink and the countertops. Everything was dry. The wine glasses wouldn't be for long.

She wouldn't wake Sam Jean yet; he was well along with sleep and sunk deep in the blood orange-colored cushion of his easy chair. He took to sleeping in that chair more than in his bed these days; usually with the radio on—the talk radio kind. It was always tuned to the AM dial and it stayed on from dawn to dusk. Sam liked the talk but hated the commercials; he would always yell that the breaks were way too long and that he would never buy the horseshit they were peddling anyway. He threatened to change the station the entire time, but it never happened. Dezzy was never sure he really even listened to the programming or if he just liked the voices talking through the fuzz of the half-shorted speakers of his thirty-year-old stereo. Dezzy noticed it too: there was a bass, a warmth, and a rhythm to the sometimes long, sometimes short sentences the hosts spat between the endless commercial breaks. While the commercials were a bore, the time spent just listening to the cadences coming across the frequency made the corporate part not so bad.

The portable radio Dezzy gave Sam was set on the coffee table in front of him with the volume turned almost all the way down. It buzzed and popped with static and what sounded like voices. She leaned in so she could hear what they were saying, but it was too low. The urge to raise the volume so she could hear what they were saying came and went. It was better not to. There were still a few things to get to in the apartment and she could get it all done faster if he wasn't yelling this and that through puffs of pipe smoke and sips of twelve-dollar red wine.

The sun had been blotted out by a passing cloud for what seemed like a long time, but as Dezzy lifted her head up toward the window, the cloud moved off and the sunlight came back through the white sheer drapes. The light filtered through and lit up the living room, illuminating a row of picture frames mounted above Sam and his easy chair. Dezzy had seen them a hundred thousand times, but each time she noticed they were there, she would examine them up close. They were photographs of various times and years throughout Sam's life: here was young Sam standing on a stoop in what looked to be Gravesend in Brooklyn; young man Sam posing with his brother Harold and their two flukes on a pier near what must be Jamaica Bay; a still-young Sam and two blonde girls dressed in formal wear outside Bond 45 restaurant in Times Square; what must have been an almost forty-year-old Sam in the driver's seat of the city bus that he drove for thirty years; another of Sam about the same age standing outside of the Hilltap Tavern in Ridgewood with brother Harold, smoking a cigarette and holding a newspaper; and the final photo was a black-and-white one of an old woman with her hair done up in bobby pins standing over what must have been a large roasted thanksgiving turkey and two small children standing close to her side. Dezzy didn't know who she was and Sam always told her it was none of her business.

Dezzy laughed to herself. Why hang a picture on the wall for others to see if you don't want those you invite into your home to know who they are?

She paused and thought about it. Perhaps he didn't invite anyone else in his home. Maybe that's why he didn't worry about explaining anything. Maybe it was just her and Sam.

The wine would decide that later, she thought.

Dezzy leaned even more over Sam—taking care not to touch him—and examined the woman's face again; the eyes were dark and the smile was only half-made, but the strength in her cheeks is what had always stood out. Dezzy's Momma had those cheeks. High, pronounced, dark, and true. Dezzy imagined this was Sam's mother. It must be. There was a strength there that could only come with the passage of years, and when Sam spoke of her, he spoke of her endurance; he spoke of it well. The cheeks stayed strong when her two young bellwether boys bled her heart dry when they didn't come at night, when a doomed marriage she didn't understand eventually took away their father, when a slew of transient boys she took up with after her husband disappeared refused to even consider a role as dad, when apartment roaches outstayed their infiltration, when the arthritic fingers ached from the thread machines in the Queens factories. Dezzy thought of the strength it took to take on the slow approach to midnight on Cypress Avenue.

She panned her eyes across the pictures again. There were no pictures of an old Sam. No one hangs old pictures of themselves. Those would stand as a visual reminder of gone youth, of sickness setting in, of time running out.

Getting old was never Dezzy's plan; getting old is slowly moving terminal cancer. The old Sam sat in the old chair in front of her asleep in a fading apartment. He could live that way forever. Dezzy didn't mind at all. She would never find the froth of older age. Here and now was it. This was heaven, and a safe heaven at that. This was Sam's gift to her and payment was only a few pours of wine, one or two grabs of outdated tabloid papers, and a smattering of dishwashing.

Dezzy wished to know who the lady in the black-and-white photograph was. Asking the young Sam Jean in the other pictures would have been the easiest way. This Sam Jean didn't like to talk about much of anything, especially not the past.

The radio buzzed and fizzed again, this time louder than before. Sam Jean opened his eyes.

"You gonna stop hanging over me and pour a glass of wine for us both?"

Dezzy leaned back and smiled.

"Have a nice nap?"

"No. Once you pour the wine, go sit on that white rug right in front of me and maybe I will. And raise the volume on the radio before you do, please. I want to hear who's spouting off for a bit."

Dezzy looked over her shoulder.

"You really want me drinking red wine on this white rug?"

"Why not? All the red wine I have ever seen you drink has gone to one place."

He pointed to her belly.

"Here?"

"There. Not a drop on your lip or your chin. One sip after the other straight down into that gut."

Dezzy petted the white rug. It was soft and the threads sifted through her fingers like white beach sand. She looked up at Sam.

"Is this new?"

"Newer than you and way newer than me."

"Where did it come from?"

"Some horseshit mail catalogue."

"Nothing attached to this? No sentimental thing or past life or love?"

Sam reached down and turned up the volume of the portable radio. It was playing a commercial.

"Shit," he muttered and lowered it back down.

Dezzy put her hand on his shoulder. "I'll get the wine."

"You should have done that five minutes ago."

"You were asleep five minutes ago."

Sam waved his hands at her in disgust. Dezzy was accustomed to this routine; she waited a moment before producing the wine from the fridge and filling the already set-out glasses.

"I put out the glasses an hour ago when I got here. I was just waiting for you to wake up. This wine doesn't have to breathe, Mister Jean."

"There you go again. There you go again with that 'Mister Jean' thing. What's it going to take for you to call me Sam and Sam only; a swift kick in the ass?"

"No no…. Maybe if you throw me out of here for good and all, Mister Jean."

Dezzy handed Sam a full glass of wine and sat cross-legged on the white rug. Sam drained the entire glass and winced. Dezzy stood up, refilled it for him, handed it back, and sat back down. Sam smiled.

"What the shit would I do without you, Dezzy?"

"You'd be okay, Mister Jean."

Sam whacked his hand across the table and sent the portable radio crashing into the wall. It didn't break but instantly shut off when the batteries popped out of the back and scattered around the living room carpet. Dezzy stood up.

He knew he frightened her. Sam brought his fist to his face and bit the knuckles before he spoke. "I'm sorry. I'm sorry, kid. Please sit down...sit back down on the rug or wherever you want. I didn't mean to do that."

"I don't like stuff like that, Mister Jean."

"I don't either. I just have been feeling my age recently and all these damn commercials playing on the radio. It's just that, well, lately, I have been looking back on my life and seeing only gray, you know what I am getting at?"

Dezzy slowly sat back down on the rug and grabbed her wine glass. "I know."

"It's been this day. All gray. All gray since you left, see? This morning with Fran yelling at me and acting like she was the warden at an old age home and I don't know any better. I don't know why I know if you'll understand, but it's just the whole undertow of this place. The reasons to leave here always outweigh everything else, yet still here I am, seventy years later, same arrangement in my apartment drinking bad wine with a person...."

Sam looked up at Dezzy. Her ponytail rested on her right shoulder as she swirled the wine in her glass. She was a girl. A baby at that.

"Why are you here, Dezzy?"

The spinning wine slowed and stopped. Dezzy took a drink. It wasn't much but it was enough to be able to answer Sam.

"I want to be here."

Sam leaned forward and shook his head.

"You could be anywhere right now. You're thin and tanned with a smile to set bridges. Oh, and don't forget that head on your shoulders." Sam looked his own body over before he continued.

"See, I am an old bloated reticent son of a bitch who sits here pointing fingers and holding endless grudges. I am not a role model. It's a godsend I don't have kids, or at least kids that I know about. I am not someone to love or to know or to give a shit about on a rainy day. What I am saying is that you look at me like I am a saint. You keep coming by here with your 'Mister Jean' routine, drinking my wine and hoping for salvation. I tell you there is none for you here, kid."

"I don't believe that, Mister Jean."

"Bah!" Sam waved his hands at Dezzy and reached for his wine. A few beams of sun came and set on the blood-orange easy chair. It set the fabric ablaze.

"See, Mister Jean? It's not all gray. The sun has found its way to you, just like I found my way to you."

Noticing the sun, Sam tried to brush it off the easy chair like dust. No dice.

"The sun is as stubborn as you are, Dezzy baby."

She didn't answer him but kept her face down, staring into the wine glass. Her reflection stared back at her, reddened and dark against the rouge liquid. A face with a half-closed mouth and wide eyes were set into a girl that looked vaguely familiar, so familiar if one just gave a second look. The face was twenty-three years old. She sighed into the glass and her breath displaced the wine, distorting her reflection with one big, quick ripple. Just like that all can change. Just like a fire makes everything malleable. It all can end so abruptly. She lifted her head and licked her lips before she spoke.

"I just saw my face—well, the reflection of my face—in the wine and I thought about how much it has changed in the last three years of me coming here. You're right when you say I could be anywhere. When I left here today, I was anywhere. No one cared if I came or went; I was an unnecessary piece of the scenery. The moment I stepped out of this place, your place, I was anywhere again. I was without a father again, I was back searching for pocket change to pay for drugs, and I was another part of the avenue that could be as unnecessary as a broken Johnny pump or a sewer grate."

She paused and looked around the apartment, smiling as she did.

"Here I do the dishes. I water your plants. I pour red wine. You talk and I laugh, sometimes I even think to myself that some of the things you say are just so that I will correct you. All your 'Fat Fran's' and 'horseshit this and that' and me telling you it isn't that way. Just like today, and all the gray you feel around you. There's the sun, Mister Jean, right there in your lap. I just was helping you see it. I was here, not anywhere. I was needed, not unnecessary. Three years earlier and right outside that door, my face was just another unnecessary one among all the others. That's why I am here."

The wine had settled back in the glass and Dezzy's reflection returned. "And I don't even want to know why you allow me to keep coming back here; I don't even need to know so don't feel you have to tell me, okay? I just want to keep it this way for as long as this way can be kept. Okay?"

Another passing cloud erased the sunlight from the easy chair and the apartment.

Sam smiled. "I'm a son of a bitch, I'm telling you."

"You are a nice son of bitch, though." Dezzy picked up his portable radio and put back the fallen batteries. It buzzed and immediately went back on to the talk station he had been listening to for months.

It was on a commercial. Sam and Dezzy laughed at the same time.

"Typical horseshit, Mister Jean?"

Sam nodded. "Typical horseshit. Now sit back down on the rug there. Can't stand people hovering around me."

Before sitting back down, she leaned over him and plucked the frame with the black-and-white photograph off the wall and placed it in Sam's lap. Dezzy backed away and sat back down on the rug.

"Who is she, Mister Jean?"

Sam stared at the frame for a moment before turning it photo-side-down in his lap.

"None of your business."

"Is she your mother?"

"Let me tell you a little something, Dezzy baby. There are a few things you should know about me—well, about most men—but mostly me."

Dezzy crossed her legs on the white rug and sipped her wine.

"Oh yeah? Then can we talk about the photograph?"

"No, we cannot. Now I know I you think me a cuddly old bastard who only talks a lot of guff to everything and everyone he loathes in the outside world but doesn't do a goddamn thing about it. By looks, although it hurts my heart to admit it, you'd be right. In the reality of it, you'd be wrong. I know I have lost a step or two in the years since those pictures above my head there were snapped, but that don't mean when I say to you that I don't want to discuss something, and you continue to ask and keep pushing me, that I won't come over there and slap the taste out of your mouth so you don't ask me again. Real men think that in their heads, even if they don't ever get up and carry it out. To further the point, they think that way especially when what they don't want to talk about has to do with their mother." Sam leaned closer to Dezzy as he brought the wine to his lips. "Do you understand?"

"My mother tried to hit me with a greasy spatula today so I think I understand. You old people are crazy. And I don't have any more room left to deal with this kind of crazy today."

Dezzy stood up and headed to the apartment door. As she went to grab the handle there was a knock.

Through the peephole she could see Fran holding a broom outside of the door.

"Well, who is it?"

"It's Fran."

"Oh no, not her."

Two more knocks came on the door.

"What do you want to do, Mister Jean?"

"I suppose you have to answer it; she can already hear us in here. Just open it up so I can get her horseshit over with."

Dezzy nodded, unlocked the chain, and opened the door. Fran looked her up and down and shook her head.

"Is Samuel here?"

"He's behind me, in the chair."

"I'm here in the chair, Fran, whaddya want?"

Fran pushed passed Dezzy and walked into the living room. When she made it to Sam she shook her head at him as well.

"You need to open a window in here! All that pipe tobacco and wine, it stinks like a roadhouse in here!"

"I like it this way."

Fran swayed the broom back and forth on the floor, scattering some dust toward the apartment entrance.

"And aren't you supposed to be working today driving that cab?"

"Tonight. And no, I am not going in tonight."

"What about you, Dezzy, why are you still here?"

Sam Jean got up out of the easy chair and grabbed the broom out of Fran's hands.

"Never mind Dezzy or my work schedule. Just tell me what you want."

Fran snatched the broom back from Sam and swept the rest of the dust and dirt into the hallway.

"Well, if you weren't sitting up here stewed on wine with a window closed you probably would have heard the sirens and maybe even the gunshot."

"There are always sirens around here. Sometimes even a gunshot or two. Worm keeps turning, Fran."

Dezzy had heard the sirens before she nodded out in Pip's car. Like Sam, she didn't pay much mind to the everyday sounds and scenery of Cypress Avenue.

"Worm keeps turning? Well get a load of this: those sirens were ambulance sirens and they were rushing to Ben Zogby's home."

Sam sat back down and grabbed the glass of wine. "So?"

"So it seems he went into a rage or something on his stoop and killed himself in front of two young girls. Word is going around one of the girls was his niece."

Dezzy brought her hands to her mouth in shock. "Oh my god—Lorraine?"

Fran swept a little more around the doorway, shaking her head as she went.

"Yes. Lorraine and her little girlfriend. Did you know them, Dezzy?"

"They were in my school, a grade or two behind me. They were always together. I just can't believe it. Are they okay?"

"Well, I was told they took off running right after it happened. No one has heard from them since."

The apartment got quiet for a moment. Then Sam spoke. "How do you know this?"

"Oh, Father John White was making his rounds in the neighborhood today and he stopped by the stoop. He told me all about it. He said that there is going to be a meeting tonight at the bar to discuss what to do with the body. Rumor is his sister don't want anything to do with him since he offed himself in front of little Lorraine. And his two kids are dead so…." Her voice trailed as she walked through the door with her broom. "Just thought you might want to know since you and Zogby used to be friendly."

Sam stood up and followed Fran in the hall. Their voices echoed as they spoke. A couple of apartment doors opened a crack to listen.

"Which bar is everyone meeting at tonight?"

"Father says the Blue Collar Bum bar or whatever you all call it."

"Did he say what time?"

"He said very late. He might have said after eleven."

"I see. Okay, thank you Fran."

"When we were younger we used to call it the Glenlo Tavern. Now they changed the name and I don't know why. I never understood why people change a good name to…."

Sam closed the door on Fran. He already had enough of her yammering. The news of Zogby's death spun in his mind and it frightened him. Is this what life was? A long day's night that ended with a heart attack or a bullet in the head?

Sam had known Zogby for years. They were around the same age. Every other morning they would meet at the Te-amo tobacco shop and talk about women and the lottery. Zogby was the one person Sam could stomach in the neighborhood. What went wrong? Everything seemed fine the last time at the shop, but that was a few months ago. He had been sending Dezzy for the tobacco in his place. He would never know what changed.

He returned the chain lock to its former position. The photograph of his mother with the turkey was still lying face down on the easy chair. Sam picked it up, returned it to the wall above his easy chair, and fell back into the cushions. Dezzy was waiting. She handed him a full glass of wine and returned to her crossed-leg position on the white carpet. Sam looked up at her.

"What's the point, Dezzy?"

"What do you mean?"

"I mean we are living our lives, all of us, like a car stuck running in place. I haven't thought of it until now, but maybe we are living life just like a car riding in neutral; moving through the round of the Earth under the control of something else until, under no power of your own, you crash dead. Seventy years of living and it just came to me."

"Well, Zogby didn't think that way."

Sam turned his head slowly to Dezzy and stared her down.

"Do you want the way out, Zogby's way out, to be the one thing you have control of?"

Dezzy took a huge sip off of the wine. "I don't know, Mister Jean."

"Me neither, kid."

"Maybe we should go to the bar tonight, you know, the meeting, to find out what really went on."

"Maybe."

"You sure, Mister Jean?"

Sam nodded and turned up the radio.

Commercials. Nothing but goddamn commercials.

evangeline

Lolly and Lorraine had finally stopped running. It was time to catch their breath and take to hiding. The girls hadn't spoken about anything since it happened, but they felt safe now. Lorraine had followed Lolly through the streets away from Zogby's apartment; they had zigzagged through Ridgewood, staying off the main avenues—especially Cypress Avenue—until they crossed the Penny Bridge and reached the entrance to the freight train tracks. These were the same tracks they walked to get to Zogby's apartment. When they reached the gray gravel and steel rails, they ran in the opposite direction from which they originally came and headed in the direction of Brooklyn. Refuge came by means of a long, dark, graffiti-covered tunnel. It was cooler in the dark it provided, but the air was stagnant, carrying the faint scent of creosote. Outside of the sound of water dripping from a leak in the concrete roof of the tunnel, it was very quiet. They would be safe here.

Lorraine loved the remote tracks but always feared being run over by a train. Lolly always reassured her, saying that the freighters came only twice a day through these tracks and never in the afternoon. There was more to fear from the transients and devil worshippers than the locomotives, she always said. Lolly believed her temporarily. She always trusted people more than machines, even the weirdos and devil worshippers. After all she witnessed today, she wasn't so sure who or what she trusted anymore.

Lorraine was sitting with her face resting on her knees, her hands still trembling, when Lolly came up to her and licked her thumb.

"You have blood on your face and in your hair, Lorraine. Jesus, let me get this off you." Her thumb gently scrubbed the dried blood away from her eyes and off of her cheeks. Lorraine didn't react to any of it.

"We are going to be okay, Lorraine. We are safe here." She continued to groom her friend's face and hair. "And don't you worry about the train coming through here, remember what I told you? It has to be about three or four in the afternoon now, the next train won't roll through until midnight."

Lorraine kept her eyes and face forward. The dripping water turned louder and the creosote scent turned into a stench. The overgrowth of wild, green, freight-train flora seemed to grow and reach out to the girls' hiding place; it too had its own leafy, musty smell and it filled Lorraine's nostrils. Her eyes darted and noticed a snake slithering through the weeds near the tracks; it hissed as it went. Large mosquitos appeared from rain puddles and took flight circling Lorraine, buzzing and landing over and over again. The tunnel seemed to grow darker now, maybe they were not safe after all, maybe a train would come. They couldn't hide out in the tracks forever. What about school and English class where they were just learning the basics of good poetry? Lorraine bit her thumb nail as a deep fear blocked everything else out: what will Mom do to me when I get home?

Lolly took her trembling hand and squeezed it. The quiet returned. Lorraine looked at her.

"Lorraine. You are going to be okay."

"I don't know, I don't know, Lolly…."

"I do, and it's going to be okay."

A car rushed by overhead and blew its horn. The sound screamed at and then away from them; immediately Lorraine thought of school and science class where they had learned about the Doppler shift. Red and blue shift meant something was louder as it approached and softer as it departed. School! What about going back to school!

"We have to get out of here Lolly; for good. I mean it. I don't want to…. I won't be able to go home or look at this place, or school, or street corners, or Cypress Avenue ever again."

"I know."

"I just want to walk these tracks straight away from here."

"We can. We will."

"My mother, Lolly, my mother. What will she think?"

Lolly pulled Lorraine's face close to hers and rested her forehead against it; the tears were hot and damp against her cheek. Lolly had her own hot tears but held them back; she knew Lorraine's would contain enough sorrow and fear from the day to wet both of their faces.

Through a cracked, broken voice, Lorraine spoke. "Why would he do this, Lolly?"

"He was a troubled old man."

"Why would he do this to me?"

"Perhaps because no man is innocent?"

Lorraine pulled away and laughed. It was the wish to have that phrase, her uncle's commentary on men, tattooed on her body that brought them under the dark of the trestle and to this moment. Lolly grinned and helped her friend to her feet.

"See, you don't need anything inked on your body for that saying to be true. You lived through it, baby!"

Lorraine rubbed her hands on her belly and fingered her navel. "I still want that tattoo."

"I still want you to get that tattoo. Never saw anyone get tattooed before. And why couldn't we? We can still get it later on, right?"

"I don't know. What are we gonna do, Lolly?"

"We'll do just what you said."

Lorraine stood puzzled. "What did I say?"

Lolly adjusted her hair into a ponytail. "We will leave here and never come back."

A rush of energy and anticipation came across Lorraine's face. "We can't really do that, can we?"

"We can and we will, if you start walking with me. You know I ain't going without you."

Lorraine kicked some of the gravel and laughed as she wiped away what was left of the tears that soaked her eye lashes. "But what about our family and school and everything else?"

Lolly had moved deeper into the trestle, inspecting the graffiti that had decorated the walls; the artists spray-painted as far as the sunlight would reach. The last tags marked where the almost complete darkness would begin. She ran her hands over the large colorful pieces; it ranged in color from baby blue with a cherry red outline to lime green and charcoal black and yellow highlights. The tags were the work of young masters, all created by her older brother Javier and his friends. Lolly fiercely loved Javier, and in the blues and reds she saw the outline of his face. They shared a room until he became a teenager, but he had already been practicing his art since he could steady a pencil. On the edge of his bed, she and Javier would sit, his hand sketching out his latest idea, with delicate true strokes, to loose-leaf paper. When the outline was done, he'd turn to her and ask what colors he should use to fill it with. Cherry red and baby blue, she'd always say. The caps would pop off and Javier would make those markers work the paper; their ink stunk up the room. Lolly loved the smell; it provided a three-second high. Javier lived in the high, three seconds at a time, as he practiced the graffiti day and night. The next day, the work was started, after the morning freight train chugged by and cleared the trestle; the boys would drink their beers and practice their infant ideas quietly on the barren walls in the underworld of the freight lines. The drained beer bottles and empty spray cans that littered their feet were covered in a small dotted wash of multicolored spray point. It was art and it was heaven. One day after Javier came home he said he wished he could spray every tunnel in the world with his tag in baby blue and cherry red; that way he and Lolly could be everywhere at once.

'The last day of school, two months ago exactly, he went to the tracks, hopped a passing train, and never came back.

"My family is my brother and what is left of him is spray-painted here on these walls. All I need to do is visit the tracks when I miss him. He is out here somewhere. Mom and Dad won't even know I am gone."

"What about my mom?"

"Your mom is going to blame you—you know that. And we are going to have to go to the cops and relive this whole damn thing." Lolly pointed to the graffiti on the wall. "See what this says?"

Lorraine came closer and struggled to see in the half-light. They were deep in the trestle tunnel now. "Yes."

"Read it, baby."

"Out loud?"

"Duh."

"Okay. It's hard to see. Okay. I think it says, 'Silently, one by one, in the infinite meadows of heaven, blossomed the lovely stars, the forget-me-nots of the angels.'"

Lolly smiled. "Sound familiar?"

"It's poetry, right?"

"Duh. We learned it this year in our modern poetry class. It's Longfellow's poem 'Evangeline.'"

"Yeah, I remember something about that name. I love the title, 'Evangeline.' Why is it on the wall here?"

"My brother added it to one of the last pieces of graffiti he did before he split. It's a beautiful line and beautiful of him to commit it forever in paint to the wall. After I read him the poem and told him how much it meant to me, he promised to add it to his next piece."

Lorraine picked up a smattering of gravel from the tracks and threw it into the flora. Two birds immediately jettisoned into the air and disappeared into the overworld.

"Mister O'Reilly taught us that poem. He went on and on about Longfellow and 'Evangeline.'"

Lolly stepped back from the wall and sat down on one of the steel rails of the tracks. She patted the rail with her hand and nodded at Lorraine to sit next to her.

The sunlight split the two girls as they sat side by side: Lorraine in the sun light and Lolly in the trestle gray.

"You know, I went on and on about 'Evangeline' because that poem is so me and you."

Lorraine smiled the smile of naivety. Lolly grabbed her hand.

"Remember when we first became friends and we stopped talking after you ditched me for the popular kids in school?"

"Oh god, not this again, Lolly."

"No, no. I don't care about it anymore."

"Good, because I don't want to have to go through making it up to you again. I swear I'll run right back to Cypress Avenue if I have to do that again!"

The girls both giggled. Lolly went on. "Well, when you were gone, it was like we lost each other. I knew you really still wanted to be my friend, which of course I made you explain and admit to me over and over again, ha ha ha. You were gone one way and I was gone the other, just like the poem. In the poem Evangeline loses Gabriel even though they want to be together. In the poem it's the great upheaval. Well, we had our own great upheaval, right?"

Lorraine smiled. She gripped Lolly's hand tighter.

"And then we were always around each other but never able to really hang during freshman year because of all of that, just like Evangeline and her man. See she was searching for Gabriel in the poem and he was always just out of reach just like us: me searching for you and you searching for me. It took us some time, but here we are now with the railroad tracks before us; one going back the way we came and the other onto the rail and roadways we have yet to explore. I heard you before. You want to leave here; all of this Cypress Avenue shit, because that's what it is—you want to leave it behind and never come back."

Lolly looked around and smiled.

"Well, here we are Lorraine; our butts sitting on the rail steel and the track boards warm beneath our sneakers with two choices: the way forward or the way backward."

A tear rolled down Lorraine's cheek. She turned to Lolly and nodded.

"I remember that poem now. In the end, Gabriel dies, doesn't he."

"Yes, he does."

"I don't want that poem to be about either of us, Lolly."

"It won't be. I said the poem is so me and you, not *exactly* me and you. We are girls. We can have it all and leave that other shit behind."

Lorraine laughed as Lolly rose, pulling her up with her. She licked her thumb again and wiped the dried salt and dirt crust the tears left around Lorraine's eyes.

"Come on, let's start walking."

"Are we really going to do this?"

"It's either this or we end up exactly the way like Long-fellow wrote 'Evangeline' to end."

Lorraine looked back into the dark of the tunnel and tried to make out the quote from 'Evangeline.' She could barely see it scribbled above the other graffiti, but she knew it was there. Above, in the overworld, a police siren sounded in the distance; its pulse echoed off the half-broken grey concrete walls and into the darkness that sat in the middle of the tunnel. Perhaps that siren was headed to her uncle's apartment building. It might just wait there to question her about her role in this whole thing. If she didn't give the right answers, then what? What would happen to her? Would she have to identify her uncle's body? Touch his hand or the gun he used on himself hours earlier? She would never do any of that. No, there was nothing left on Cypress Avenue for her or for Lolly. Javier made it out. Lolly wanted to make it out, too. Her mother would one day understand.

Lorraine grabbed Lolly's hand and started running towards the soon-to-be-setting sun; the steel rails lit bright and shined with the hope of an evening freight train, maybe even the one Javier found on his way out, to be waiting for them in Brooklyn. Maybe that train would be decorated with the cherry red and baby blue markers Javier made just for Lolly and now, for Lorraine too. Everything was ahead of them.

A new tattoo idea came to Lorraine as the wind rushed through her hair. It would be in black script ink as Javier had spray-painted on the trestle wall and run the length of the arm:

Silently, one by one, in the infinite meadows of heaven,

Blossomed the lovely stars, the forget-me-nots of the angels.

Behind them, Cypress Avenue took in the oncoming dusk. The oranges and reds began to seep across the horizon and into the side streets of the neighborhoods. Ridgewood was ablaze in the first circle of hell that had greeted Dante and Virgil.

PART 6

War

Ms. Madre's feet shuffled as she slowly brought the tea kettle to the table and set it on the half-folded dishtowel that was there to keep the hot pot from burning through the plastic tablecloth. The tablecloth was one of a dozen blue plaid tablecloths Ms. Madre kept on hand at the apartment. She stacked them neatly in the closet with the dishtowels and sewing thread. They cost a dollar a piece at the corner five and dime and she took to purchasing one every week just in case another accidental hole appeared. Ms. Madre spent a lot of time alone with the tablecloth; during the early part of the morning while sipping cups of Sanka, through the afternoon scribbling through the crossword, and on into the evening as she swallowed water pills.

The only time she left the apartment was for the mail. The mail still hadn't come today; the day she needed it to come the most. So she was back with the blue plaid tablecloth. But today she wasn't alone.

It was afternoon now and she had a visitor. Ms. Madre poured the hot tea into the cup across from her, filling it halfway. The Russian nodded his head to signal that he had enough and pulled gently on his cigar. The smoke spilled back out over his mouth like an overflowing cauldron, rippled through his thick goatee, and floated down to the tablecloth before dissipating into the apartment.

Ms. Madre put the kettle down and sat across from the Russian. She smoothed her hands across the table, feeling the plastic sheen of the tablecloth under her palms. It was cool even though the apartment was full of summertime humidity. The Russian sipped the tea and slouched back in the kitchen chair.

"Thank you, Ms. Madre."

"It's no problem."

"And thank you for inviting me in. I thought it better than us talking downstairs on the wet stoop and in the sun. It is hot as hell out there, isn't it?"

Ms. Madre nodded. "Yes, and I like it much better up here at the table anyway, it's just more comfortable."

The Russian looked around the apartment. The living room was mostly filled with brown-colored furniture, which made him feel sleepy and at ease. He noticed that the carpet, also brown, was thick and high like unmanicured, soft, dying autumn grass. Ms. Madre only kept forty- and sixty-watt light bulbs in lamps that kept the back rooms of the apartment warm in low light.

Turning back to the kitchen, the Russian noticed the stark contrast of the blues and whites that filled this room against the browns that filled the back rooms. The linoleum that covered the kitchen floor was a brilliant white, spotless and without abrasion. The countertops and cabinets were of a neon blue and they made up the area near the stove and refrigerator. The sunlight filtered through baby blue sheer drapes and tinted the sunlight with the same color as the countertops. Upon seeing the light, the Russian instantly thought of every Mary, mother of God, garden statue he had ever seen: the pale-faced, sad woman in the dress and blue mantle with her hands outstretched.

Ms. Madre coughed. She was dressed in a floral purple muumuu with black sandals strapped to her feet, and her face was made of dry olive skin and thick glasses covering a nose that hovered over the start of a mustache. Mother Mary she was not. The Russian cleared his throat after the silence. "It's a very comfortable apartment you have here."

"Yes it is."

"You seem to have put a lot of work into living here. The living room seems like a very nice place to spend one's time."

"It can be."

"Why don't we take our tea—well, your coffee and my tea—in there and talk?"

Ms. Madre smoothed her hands across the tablecloth and traced the plaid pattern with her fingertips.

"To be honest, Ivan, I spend most of my time right here. I get up in the morning and turn on that coffee pot right there." She pointed to the blue-and-chrome coffee maker on the countertop. "I let it fill the pot full of boiling water, make my Sanka, and then sit right back down here at the table."

Ivan shrugged and put the cigar back in his mouth.

"You like it here, no?" As he spoke the cigar twitched up and down in his mouth.

"Well, I've been here a long time, as you know."

"Yes, you have. My father told me all about his tenants before he passed away."

"I traveled to Brighton for the funeral."

"Yes, I remember. All of you tenants did. My father would have liked that. He liked respect and that was respectful of you all."

Ms. Madre smiled and sipped her Sanka.

Ivan shifted his position in the chair and leaned forward, laying the cigar on the end of the table; its ash end left burning and hanging off the edge. Ms. Madre turned her head to the cigar and frowned.

"You know, Ms. Madre, I have worked hard to be very much like my father. His values, his presence, his ways. They are old ways. You can relate to the old ways."

Ms. Madre nodded. Ivan sipped the tea again.

"This tea needs something. Do you have some sugar or, better yet, a little whiskey I can add to it?"

"I don't have that in the house. When my husband was alive we did, but no more."

"That's okay, Ms. Madre." Ivan reached into his black sports coat and produced a small silver flask. "I carry this around for special moments or to add to coffee or even tea or just, well, just because."

He opened the top and poured some into the tea. It fizzed and the vapor took on the smell of lemon and whiskey. Ivan winced as he drank it down. Ms. Madre hadn't noticed; she was busy watching the cigar ash grow as it sat at the edge of the tablecloth. She had twelve more just like it in the linen closet, blue plaid just the same, but this one was brand new, freshly opened from the plastic it came with just this morning. She spread it out over the kitchen table just before she went down for the mail. And to replace it again so quickly; and from another burn! Ms. Madre frowned again. Ivan noticed her displeasure and offered the flask across the table.

"Oh I am sorry, Ms. Madre, did you want some as well?"

"No thank you, Ivan. I don't drink."

"No? You drink the coffee."

"It's Sanka. And that's all I drink."

"I see, I see. Here's to your Sanka and my whiskey then!"

Ivan raised his flask and cheered the empty space between them. Ms. Madre didn't touch her Sanka. He belly-laughed after the drink found its way to his gut and sat up straight in his chair.

"So what are we going to do here, Ms. Madre?"

"First, may you please get your cigar off of my new tablecloth before you burn a hole in it?"

Ivan picked up the cigar and puffed on it. He flicked the ashes into the tea cup. "That better?"

Ms. Madre sipped the Sanka again without answering.

"Good. Now, you know I don't drive all the way from Brighton Beach often, yes?"

Ms. Madre nodded.

"I did this time because this is the third month in a row you have been late with the rent. Each month the rent comes a little later, and a little later, and here we are today again: even later. This is not a good pattern, Ms. Madre. I am now suspecting the rent might not come at all this month."

Ms. Madre shook her head back and forth. "No, it will be here. It comes in the mail. It just isn't here yet. I was waiting for the mail downstairs on the stoop all morning.

You can knock on Telly's door and ask him, he was with me. It just hasn't come yet. I am positive the check will be with the rest of the mail when the postman finally delivers it."

Ivan puffed on the cigar and placed it back on the edge of the table. "I *have* knocked on Telly's door and asked him. He said he hadn't seen you all day, Ms. Madre. It's funny, though, his rent is late too."

Ms. Madre had forgotten. She knew Telly was young and scared. It was no wonder he lied. He wasn't a bad kid, he was the only son of a mother who one day came into a small inheritance and up and left him in the apartment they both shared since he was a little boy. She left a note on the table that said she had paid Ivan's father full rent for three years and left her son enough money to buy food and drink for the same amount of time. Then she was gone with a one way ticket to Miami, Florida; her dream was to live on the beach and eat clams until she could no longer take the sun or stare at another shell. Four weeks later her body was fished out of a water canal by the local police near Pompano Beach. Ms. Madre intercepted the telegram one morning that came from the drug dealer Telly's mother had moved in with when she first got to Miami. The message explained everything. It ended saying the reason he sent it was because the last time they spoke, Telly's mother told him should anything happen to her that they should send word to her only son in New York. Ms. Madre never told Telly. She knew he would never have understood. That was just over three years ago. Now the rent was due.

"He must have misunderstood you. I was down there. There's been no mail delivered here all day. As soon as it gets here I will get the rent to you. You father always understood."

Ivan hit the flask again and picked the cigar up; the hot ash fell to the tablecloth and sat there. Ms. Madre immediately wiped it away and onto the floor. The grey ash dispersed across the white linoleum like cremated remains cast across the sea.

"Uh oh, the tablecloth, I forgot. I am truly sorry, Ms. Madre." Ivan lit the end of the cigar again and sucked on it gently as he waited for a response.

It never came.

"My father used to tell stories during the holidays, yes?"

Before she could answer Ivan got into it. "Let me tell you a little story. That's how my father would begin, right? Of course, let me tell you a little story. When my parents first came to this country from the Ukraine, my father was a woodsman and lumberjack married to a seamstress who only mended his clothes. You see, she wasn't much of a seamstress, more of someone who knew how to finger a needle and a thread the right way to keep my father's socks intact. Immediately after deboarding the ship that had taken him and my mother to America, every Russian went to Brooklyn and those who were unlucky made it to Brighton Beach. Let me tell you about Brighton Beach! In those days, well, plainly said, it sucked, Ms. Madre!" Ivan laughed as he spoke. He took a sip and continued on.

"So my mother went to a factory and my lumberjack father was on a beach. What could he do? There wasn't a tree for miles. He did what many unemployed Russians did while not working; he spent many evenings in the Russian taverns and clubs that outlined our area to live in. That's when my mother got pregnant with me. You know we never

left that area, Ms. Madre, not once. I grew up thinking that
the entire world was the neighborhood of sand and ocean
and tan-colored, tall high-rises. My father would come
home stinking of the bar most days. Then most nights.
You know what I asked myself the most, Ms. Madre?" Ivan
drank deeper on the flask this time.

"No."

"Right! No! How could you know? I haven't told you
yet. Well, here it goes. I asked myself, 'Self, Father is very
drunk, how do you think he feels knowing his little son is
seeing him drunk like this?' I knew he was very drunk. Hell,
the very drunk neighborhood knew he was very drunk, too.
That's why I hated that neighborhood; my mother did, too.
Even Father hated it in the end. He drank more because
they gave him more drink. He didn't want it. But some
stupid so-and-so would show up with a cup of this and that.
There was no care for the little boy or the woman at home
he had to return to after another day of not finding work in
the trees or the seas; no, he had to drink. That's when he left
my mother and went to live under the goddamn boardwalk!
The Brighton Beach boardwalk! He left us with nothing.
My father! Your understanding landlord! Hahahaha."

Ivan slapped his knees and gritted his teeth, laughing
through spit and whiskey.

"Here's where it gets good, Ms. Madre. This is the
part where my mom and I get folded back in. I hated my
father for years. But one day he apologized and made things
right. My mother was an angel, so of course she accepted
his apology and let him come home. All I wanted to know
to accept his apology was why he had left us in the first

place. Simple request, right? Not asking too much, right, Ms. Madre? Well, this is what he told me. While spending his time under the boardwalk and refusing to divorce my mother—who, by the way, still had to continue working at the factory all day and night—he says he met a man, a soothsayer or a magician, something like that. They drank and laughed it up for days before one day, the man got serious. He says the man told him to leave Brighton Beach and find his way to Wall Street, that they had endless piles of money and that there would be work there. So, he left again, this time from under the boardwalk, and found work on Wall Street."

"I never knew any of this Ivan."

"He didn't tell you this one, did he? Well, one Christmas, he was a janitor in a large firm's building—imagine using those big strong axe-wielding arms to push around a mop or a broom? But there he was, my father, the Russian lumberjack, pushing a broom, going up and down the halls. Let me tell you Ms. Madre, he kept the place immaculate and he treated everyone with respect, even love."

"He did that here, too; treated everyone with love and respect."

"Love and respect, right. Let me finish. As my father told it, late one evening he was alone working late in the building. From out of the darkness, a young, attractive woman appeared and began talking to him. Now, my father hated women unless they were there to screw him, you see? His love was mostly being tolerant, you see. He tolerated my mother and hated women. Sex was sex, he had no interest in talking to the women he was about to screw. He was full of respect, ha ha ha! Anyway, this woman stopped him, and of course he immediately hated her until she knew who he was; she knew about his time under the boardwalk, she knew about his family, and most everything else about him. He became frightened, but she told him not to be, that she had a message for him from the man my father met during his stay under the boardwalk. It was written on a folded piece of paper that she handed to him. Then, just like how she came to him, the woman disappeared back into the dark. Needless to say, my father was really scared now, so he got the hell out of there and went back to his apartment. There he read the note. It was a financial tip to invest every last dollar he had in some unknown stock that was about to make a huge splash and go public in the coming week. Being that the man under the boardwalk was right about Wall Street, my father did as the note said. By the end of the week, the stock split not once, but three times. The dividends came tenfold and it gave my father the balls to come back to Brighton and to me and Mother. He was a success now and he showered everyone in the neighborhood with drinks and food, even gifts. For us, he gave little more than the equivalent of the American IOU."

Ivan sipped on the flask and put the cigar back down on the edge of the table. This time Ms. Madre didn't frown.

"He took the IOU money, moved Mother and I out of Brighton, and bought this building. You know the rest about this place."

"Yes I do, thank you. Interesting history of your father, most of which, Ivan, I never knew."

Ivan stood up and kicked the chair behind him.

"You know, I hate IOUs."

Ms. Madre knew what the thump of the chair meant; she just hadn't seen or felt it for a while. In her younger years she'd kicked her own chair backward and stood up to face the blundering idiot, whoever they happened to be. Now, she was tired. The afternoon waned and the postman hadn't yet arrived. Ms. Madre knew now he never would. The heat had grown in the apartment since Ivan walked through the front door and Ms. Madre began to sweat. She wasn't sure it was the sun or the furnace but that heat had to end. This all had to end.

Church bells gave their hymn and belled the three o'clock chime. Ms. Madre placed both hands on the tablecloth and pushed her body up. Below her face lie the plaid blue pattern, untainted and smooth, glowing with the penetrating blued sunlight.

Ivan took his cigar and put it out into the tablecloth. "You hear me, Madre, I want the rent. I have dicked around long enough with your tea and tablecloth."

The cigar burned through the plastic and stuck into the elder wood. She nodded and picked herself up from the kitchen chair. "I hear the bells of Aloysius. It's three o'clock. I will check the mailbox again. It's bound to be there." A pain shot her down her legs and pooled in her feet. Each step felt like static electricity.

Ivan took a pull on his flask. "Go ahead. You go see. In ten minutes be back up here with the check for me or start packing your stuff."

Ms. Madre didn't respond as she passed through the apartment door and into the stairwell. Betty's door was shut and her apartment was silent. Maybe she was gone for the day. That would be good. It appeared that the banging Ms. Madre had done on the wall had settled whatever had occurred earlier in the day.

Ms. Madre's hip buckled a bit through each step. She made it to the top of the staircase and saw Betty crouched and sobbing on the floor. Next to her on the bottom stair was a young girl on bended knee, praying with her eyes to heaven. There was always a girl on the bottom stair; sometimes asleep sometimes sobbing. Ms. Madre called to Betty as she made her way down the steps. "Betty, you all right? What happened?"

Betty looked and rushed up the stars to help Ms. Madre make her way down. When they made it to the bottom she handed Ms. Madre a note. She pointed to the girl and wiped the tears from her eyes. "This girl, this goddamn creature gave me the note. She says it came from Father John White."

Ms. Madre unfolded it and read it out loud.

ZOGBY IS DEAD. HE SHOT HIMSELF THIS AFERNOON ON HIS STOOP. JUST GOT THE CALL. GUESS WE WERE A LITTLE TOO LATE IN GETTING YOU TWO TO TALKING. SAY TWENTY HAIL MARYS. FJW

Betty sniffed and another tear rolled down her eyes.

"I am so sorry, my dear. I am so very sorry. That Father John is a nasty, nasty man. I am sorry for you."

Sarah Jane stopped praying and looked up at Betty and Ms. Madre. "You shouldn't say things like that about Father John. He represents God here on earth. He is helping to fight the devil and so am I. I will pray for you both." Her eyes closed and she continued to pray.

Just then the black building door opened; it was Telly. He was holding a stack of mail. Ms. Madre could read her name scribbled on the top envelope. Telly handed it and a few other pieces to her.

"Is the Russian still upstairs, Ms. Madre?"

"Yes. He's in my apartment waiting for me to get the mail and my check and pay him the rent."

Telly smiled. "Well I have the mail, but what a crazy story. The mail was late today because it seems as if the postman just abandoned his carriage and left his job. Someone called the post office and they sent another carrier to finish his route. He just delivered our mail not ten minutes ago."

Ms. Madre thumbed through the envelopes. The check was there. In the past, it was now just a matter of her getting the money to Ivan and ushering him out of the apartment, back to Brighton Beach. That wouldn't be enough, not this time. Ms. Madre decided that he wasn't going to get the check. Ivan wasn't going to get anymore checks from anyone in the building.

"Want me to run the check up to him? I have a pen here so you can just sign it over to him," Betty reached into her pants pocket and pulled out a lighter first, then found a pen. Ms. Madre took the lighter from Betty, pushing the pen away.

"No Betty. No pen. No check. I want you and Telly to leave here, just get far away. I will take care of Ivan. I will take care of everything. Take Telly and just go now."

Betty watched as Ms. Madre shuffled her feet across the bottom-floor landing and into the hallway that led to the boiler room. A shudder came over Betty and she grabbed Telly by the hand and pulled him back a little.

"What do you mean? What are you going to do? Just give him the check. What is she going to do?" Telly's voice had the beginnings of panic.

"I think we better let her go, Telly. Let's get out of here."

"Why? What is she doing? She has the check so she can pay Ivan. What is wrong with her?"

Betty opened the door and Telly walked out ahead of her, still mumbling and questioning everything. She waited there and watched until Ms. Madre opened the boiler room door and disappeared behind it.

"I think she is going to give Ivan everything she owes him. Let's get out of here." Sarah Jane continued to pray on the bottom step, her eyes still heavenward. Betty beckoned her to follow them out of the building.

"Hey, you need to get up and get out of here. Come on." Sarah Jane didn't stir.

"Hey, you hear me? Let's go! You need to get out of here." Sarah Jane whipped her head in the direction of the doorway.

"Shhh. I haven't finished all of the Hail Marys Father John told me I had to say. I am not leaving until I am done."

"You can pray at home. You need to get out of this hallway and into the street and start heading away from here."

Sarah Jane laughed. "The street? I'm not going out there. The devil is out there. He's right outside the doorway, the one you are standing in. No, you go; I'll just say a few more Hail Marys for you." Her eyes closed and the Hail Marys continued.

Betty could wait no longer. She and Telly headed down the stoop and took off in the direction of St. Aloysius Church.

Ms. Madre flipped on the light switch. It was a dim bulb, just like the ones in her apartment. The light pleased her. Right there in front of her was the old, green, rusted boiler. Many days she'd had to go and check on it when the heat stopped working in the building and Ivan refused to come to fix it. She knew how it all worked—the pipes, the gas main, the boiler pan. Ms. Madre reached for the gas hose and unscrewed it from the boiler pipe. When the hose released, the smell of gas instantly filled the room. The light bulb flickered off for a second; the boiler room in the dark had at one time frightened her, so much that she always brought a spare light bulb with her in case the one in there burned out. No more; this time she stayed calm until the light sparked back on.

Ms. Madre coughed through the gas and made her way back to the boiler room door. A voice was yelling her name down the stairs. It was Ivan. It became louder as she opened the door and stood in the hallway.

"Madre! You get lost down there? Did the mailman come yet?"

She took the lighter and flicked it on. She called back up the stairs, answering him.

"Yes, Ivan, he did."

"Oh yeah? You got my money?"

Ms. Madre held the flame to the check. It caught fire right away.

"Yes I do, Ivan, I have it right here."

"Well come back up here and give to me, I have to get out of this hellhole and beat the traffic back to Brighton!"

Ms. Madre opened the boiler room door and tossed the burning envelope inside. She watched as it floated for a moment before falling to the ground. At once she felt faint; the opened door had allowed the natural gas to rush out and fill her nose and lungs. The large quantity of vapor overwhelmed her and she collapsed to the floor.

The boiler door slammed shut and the light from the bulb flicked off again. *So this is how it all ends,* she thought to herself.

Ivan stood in the doorway of Ms. Madre's apartment, waiting to see her slow shuffle coming back up the staircase with his money. His impatience got the best of him.

"Forget it, I'll come down to you, Ms. Madre. Just wait down there. I'll be right down." After another hit off the flask, Ivan tossed the remainder of the cigar on the floor, crushing it under his foot.

He was at the top stair when a fireball blasted through the lobby and threw him off his feet. The blast shook the building and sent the black brass door off its hinges and into the street. The ground floor was immediately engulfed with flames that quickly danced up the walls and caught onto the staircase before making their way up to the second floor.

Sarah Jane was done praying now.

And there was still no check.

This was checkmate.

BOOK III

PART 1

Stories from St. Nicholas Avenue

Brown bleat
On a bored
Brooklyn street
And we
Tongue dry and simple mind
Can fantasize and pantomime
The baptized who live on
Mushroom can—
And frozen peas—
An avenue delicacy
From the coffee cups
And Sanka grinds
To the saltwater suds
On Williamsburg rocks
To the liquor store handout
The Lady who takes and sips it too often
For the panhandle giveback

We pray and confess in playful jabs of
    pussyfoot words
The stolen swords
A baneful bunch who gather in fearful stance—
The blood below their knuckles
    clench—teeming
For a place to rest its fist
At the Transient Passerby Bum Bar
And the brown bleat
Of Himrod Street
That which runs not five miles from the dirty
    green of the East River,
It's good to these here feet
For walking
Writing
Fasting
Pacifying
And in time,
The fresh name of the Lord
Spoken on the priest's empty virgin tongue,
Feels like the life after death pitch:
To dead ones
And thin ones
Those pasted, pointed ones,
Abbreviated ill-will ones
These are the ones on that border
Cypress Avenue
St. Nicholas Avenue
The thin line
A drunken Valentine

* night *

From Brooklyn to Queens
And all the bodegas, fake Broadways, and
    ashcans in between
I'll be on the stoop on Harmon Street,
Where make out sessions are the national pass
    time
And rent checks are well overdue
By given-in postmen
And southern-born Yankee preachers
Give divine homilies
With vodka and lime
For you
And you
And she and he
Not for fresh faced little girls
Who took the freight lines far away
Or dead sons of dead inside men
Who now have to face
That dead face once again
With a baseball mitt and a heavenly grin
Just in time for the night
To begin.

how all things should end

Pat Wilson had been standing at the door of his apartment with the key in the lock for some time. The white door, worn brass lock, and gold-painted door knob stared at him. He stared back. Turning the key meant many things, things that he had been putting off for some time. *Humanity was always about being too late,* he thought. Fathers and sons, they too knew all about too late. When Pat was a boy, his father used to tell him that time waits for no man. He uttered that phrase to a young Pat Wilson often, usually right before bedtime. His father worked from dawn to dusk, Monday through Saturday, at the plant; when he came home all he wanted was his dinner, the evening edition of the paper, and then bed. Before he turned in for the night, he'd kneel down next to Pat and put his hand on his shoulder.

"Time waits for no man, Pat," he'd say. "My father told me that when I was your age and now I am telling you. Always remember that. Goodnight."

That was the daily exchange; there were very few instances of "I love you, son" or "Let's do this together, son." There was never time to throw the ball around the baseball diamond or head to an amusement park for them; it was work all week plus Saturday, and Sunday was to be reserved for the Lord. All Pat seemed to need and know from his father was that time didn't wait for men. The meaning behind the phrase eluded him and he never had the chance to ask his father to explain what it meant. There never seemed to be time; almost as soon as his father had knelt down next to him and patted him on the shoulder, he would already be off to bed. Young Pat was left slightly puzzled but happy to hear his father's voice.

One morning time ran out on Pat's father. He died in his sleep from a stress-induced heart attack when Pat was seven years old. It was then that he understood what his father had meant. It was also then the game of catch was one he would have to learn alone.

The keys still dangled in the lock. How long had he been standing there he wasn't sure, but the key had to be turned and the door opened. Contained inside there was a congestion, an ignored, heavy-on-the-lungs-and-heart congestion that was made up of equal parts loss, regret, and denial. The unlocked door meant many things; walking thought it meant facing those things. Pat gripped the doorknob tight and leaned in, but still couldn't find the courage to turn the key. Out of the corner of his eye, he could make out that the apartment door down the hall was open and there was someone standing there staring at him. Pat quickly turned his head and looked down the hall. A little blonde girl in a pink and white dress looked back.

"You have been standing there a long time," she said. "You going to stand there all day?"

Pat didn't answer. He had seen the girl before, wandering around the building—but never with her parents. She was always clean and dressed nicely, but she was always alone when he saw her. He thought her name was Greta, but he wasn't sure. A voice called her name out and told her to close the door and get back inside. Pat was right about her name. He turned back to the keys in his door lock.

"You should go inside before it's too late." Her small voice filled the hallway.

Pat turned this time full back towards Greta, but she had already disappeared behind the closing door.

He called out to her anyway. "Wait, what did you say?"

There was no response. Greta's door lock clicked and echoed, sounding like a prison cell door as the dead bolt shut. The hallway grew very silent.

Without realizing it, Pat had unlocked his own front door at the same time as Greta had locked hers. His leaning front shifted his weight and pushed open the door a little. The apartment was almost completely dark except the green light of the LED clock radio and cable box. He slowly wiped his shoes on the "Father and Son's Place. Gonna Be Dirty Anyways So Don't Wipe!" doormat. Baseball diamond sand fell of his shoes and crackled as it spilled onto the tiled floor. He always loved the way it sounded.

Pat pushed the rest of the door open and walked inside the apartment, fumbling for the light switch; it was placed next to the door in such a way that he always missed it upon first try. When he finally found it and flipped it on, two of the bulbs in the three-pronged light fixture were blown out, leaving the one remaining sixty-watt bulb the job of illuminating the room.

It didn't do much in ways of light.

"Dammit," Pat muttered. He hated the dark. The darkness meant less time for parks and play, it meant closer to lima-bean dinners and early bedtime, it meant closer to a morning that could always bring death. Pat liked daylight and always preferred taking Frankie to day ball games at Shea Stadium to see the Mets play. You could always find them in the topmost corner of the upper deck at the start of the game, but they always made it down to field level by the seventh inning. Between hotdogs and Cracker Jack and never wanting to come back, Pat and his son would yell at the pitcher if the Mets were losing or jump up and down and cheer for the batter if the Mets had the bases loaded. The chance to snag a foul ball ceaselessly excited Pat; though he had never caught one when he was a kid, he wanted badly for Frankie to have his turn at getting a hold of an authentic game ball. They both always brought their baseball gloves to the stadium, tucking them under their arms between innings. When the pitcher would go into his windup, they'd put their gloves on and wait. If the bat cracked and if the ball went foul, Pat would yell, "Ooo ooh it's coming this way!" grabbing Frankie's arm excitedly before watching the sailing ball sail away into another part of the park. Felt like a hundred miles away to Frankie. Pat never wavered; there would always been another pitch and another foul ball; especially when Darryl Strawberry came to the plate. Strawberry would foul off pitch after pitch during his at-bats. Pat knew their day would come. The next pitch and foul ball they'd both be at it again—

Father and son with their baseball mitts high in the air in hopes a foul ball would come back down to Shea Stadium from the sun.

Pat looked up to the ceiling in hopes a baseball would be coming down toward him. There was no ball, just a fading sixty-watt light bulb. Shea Stadium and the sun this was not.

The scent of bacon and eggs still hung on the air of the apartment; Frankie's plate sat in the same position Pat left it in that morning, the eggs and bacon untouched. He frowned and dumped the cold food in the garbage. Pat looked towards his son's room. His eyes squinted to adjust to the ever-present low light. The bedroom door was now open, and there, standing in its aperture, dressed in his baseball uniform and muddy cleats, was Frankie. A Louisville slugger was slumped over his right shoulder, his other hand outstretched towards his father. Pat swallowed and licked his lips. "Frankie?"

"Dad, where's my mitt?"

Pat no longer had the baseball mitt that came in the mail that morning for his son. The mitt was now where it belonged, where it needed to stay.

"I took it to the park with me, Frankie."

"Did you leave it there, Dad?"

Pat swallowed again. This time he had no spit in his mouth. "Yes, I did."

"How are we gonna break it in, Dad, if it's still at the park? I can't catch fly balls with a stiff mitt!"

"I didn't think…. I didn't know you would be able to break it in with me. So I did it for you."

"Is it the Rawlings one, brown leather with the chess-board pocket?"

"Yes. It came in the mail this morning."

"Just like Cal Ripken?"

"Yes, Frankie, just like Iron Man."

"Why don't we go get it, Dad, and play catch for a while…that's if you still need me to."

A tear rolled down Pat's cheeks and made its way to his chin. He stood motionless, staring at his son; Frankie's small frame barely filled out the uniform but he played with a smile of a thousand oceans. His arm wasn't long and his body not lanky, but he loved to play catch with his Dad out in the park or even in the lot before they went in to see the Mets play the afternoon away. It was catch Pat missed the most, catch that was most important. The passing of the white hardball back and forth between he and Frankie displaced the need to fill the air with meaningless words. It was the soft toss and slap in the mitt that meant a bond. The throw from a big arm to a little arm that meant trust. The laugh and cheer that came when one of them made a good catch or throw; that was love. It was the mitt on Frankie's hand and that little league uniform that held a hope and promise for his son to have a future and be the kind of man his own father wished he could be to a young Pat.

The tear had made its way down the length of his face formed into a drop and hung on the bottom of his chin. It fell away and dotted the kitchen floor. Looking around the apartment, all that was left were walls covered in his and his son's love for the old ball game. There were little league trophies and graying team pictures standing upright on the nailed-to-the-wall wooden shelves, as well as baseball card pictures of Frankie from when he was in the pee wee leagues, then little league, and that first year in intramurals; the year everything came to an end.

All Pat wanted was to play catch with his boy. But the glove was at the park, six feet underground.

Pat swallowed again and cleared his throat of the caught tears. "I don't think we can play anymore, son."

The smile left Frankie's face. Pat wiped his forearm across his eyes and his nose.

"I think it's time we put the ball down and call it a game."

Frankie dropped the Louisville slugger on the ground and took off his ball cap.

"You mean it, Dad?"

Pat nodded. He could no longer hold back the tears. Frankie smiled at him and turned back to his room. The door closed behind him.

The sixty-watt light bulb finally gave out. A moment of silence passed, before—from underneath Frankie's bedroom door—a yellow glow appeared and crept out into the apartment. Pat immediately fell to his knees and brought his face to the ground. He tried to look under the space between the door and the floor. It was just light. There hadn't been light in that room in years.

Jumping back to his feet, Pat moved close to the door, putting his ear up to the white-painted wood. He held his breath and listened. Nothing. No sound, no noise, nothing—just as it had been for years. However, the light still persisted from underneath the door, this time glowing even brighter and larger, almost reaching up towards him.

Pat knelt back down to the ground, his face touching the light, and whispered through the empty space between the door and the floor. "Hello?"

Silence.

"Frankie?"

The light pulsed brighter now.

"Frankie, it's Dad. Are you in there?"

The light pulsed even greater now, filling the outline of the door and blasting into the apartment. Pat pulled himself back up just as the knob turned and the door released back open. His father's voice filled his mind again: *Pat, time waits for no man.* He wouldn't wait. Pat wanted that last moment. He walked into the room and closed the door behind him without hesitation.

The room was alive. It looked just as it did when Frankie was a boy: Mets posters, Roberto Clemente posters, and a life-size Pete Rose cutout covering all four walls and above them, the team flag of every baseball team in both leagues strung around the top just like the crown of a baseball stadium. There was even the faint scent of Topps baseball card chewing gum permeating the room.

Pat spotted his son; he was still in his baseball uniform, standing near an open window that led to the fire escape. Frankie smiled at him.

"Are you sure, Dad? I can go now?"

Pat walked to his son and knelt down to the floor. He leaned his head against his sons lap.

"I don't want you to go, God no, I don't want you to go. I took your brand-new mitt with me today Frankie, and I waited for you in the park, just like always, hoping you'd come this time to throw the ball around. On my way there I told everyone who knew you how great your arm is and how much you and I were going to work hard and long to get you to the big stage. Just the thought of that has kept me alive all these years. Just the hope of that has kept me here, trying, waiting for you to, maybe, I don't even know how, but maybe for you to come back to me."

Pat wiped the tears again. He looked up at Frankie.

"So I again waited in that park—our park. I saw other kids and other dads doing what kids and dads do together. And still I waited. I threw the ball in that mitt so hard so many times that I thought it went right through the leather and came out the other side. But even that didn't change anything. Then morning became the afternoon and before I knew it, the sun was almost gone and the park was emptying out. Those same kids were leaving with their dads, leaving me just with your mitt. It was then, Frankie, that I knew—though it hurt me worse than any pain I could even imagine—that you weren't coming. That you weren't ever coming. It was also then that I realized I couldn't keep the mitt, your mitt, anymore. So, I walked out on the diamond, right at third base—the base I saw you standing at the last time we played catch, and I buried the mitt deep in the sand there. Because I thought maybe one day, if you did come back, you would go there first, right to third base and find the mitt. Then you could take the mitt and wait for me, because now, Frankie, I can no longer wait for you."

The wind kicked up and blew through the open window; the light that had kept the room in a radiant glow began filtering out through the window and up the fire escape. Frankie smiled again at his father and pulled his head close to him. Pat's tears instantly stopped.

"This is just a rain delay, Dad. I'll see you after the rain stops, and then we can finish our catch."

Frankie let go of his father's face and followed the light out of the window onto the fire escape. Pat watched as his son ascended with the light up the building and the fire escape steps until he and it disappeared into a small point, like a star in the black velvet sky.

Then the sound of thunder rolled across the darkness. A raindrop touched Pat's nose. The rain delay was underway.

PART 3

eliminent

a hard rain had been falling for hours over Ridgewood. From the kitchen window, Earl could still see
the billowing white smoke rising and coming across town
even though he was slumped in his chair. The rain came
just an hour or so too late for the fire on Himrod Street.
Everyone in the building at the time the furnace exploded
never made it out. Ma had been on the phone for hours and
always ended up getting the cord, which was extra-long so
she could wander around, wrapped around the furniture.
Ma loved to eat while gabbing on the phone. Earl didn't
mind; he had drunk enough scotch for four men that afternoon. He had a few more three-finger scotches with dinner;
a dinner that came late because Ma decided to slow-cook
the vegetables and panfry fish. Earl had eaten all the fish but
left his plate full of vegetables. Earl stared hard at the scotch
while Ma kept up with the phone.

"Oh, and they say that it might not be an accident, did
you hear that? Oh, I wonder if it was that son-of-a-gun
Russian trying to get insurance money to pay for all the
alcohol and gambling he does in Brooklyn." Ma waved a

large piece of striper on the edge of her fork back and forth while she spoke.

"No, no one survived! I heard the blast was so big and the fire so hot that they couldn't even identify the bodies! Could you imagine, oh!" She speared a potato and carrot and stuffed them in her mouth as she listened to whoever it was on the opposite end of the phone. The voice coming through the receiver was so loud that at times Earl could make out what they were saying. The voice sounded just like Ma's. He thought she might be even talking to herself on the other line.

"I know, they say it was hell on Earth! Could you even… could you even…could you imagine?"

Earl swirled the scotch around in the glass. He noticed that the apartment was very muggy and now carried the scent of salted fish, lemon, and basil. It was the rain that made it muggy, but it was Ma's cooking that made it stink. Earl liked to pan-roast the fish in butter only, but Ma always had to spice everything up. She thought life needed more spice; in food, in music, in faith—and what the salt, garlic, and herbs couldn't add in, the good Lord would.

Earl watched Ma chew another chunk of striper. The outside of the fish was cooked beautifully; lightly golden and dotted with specks of paprika, black pepper, oregano, and thyme. But on the inside, Earl knew what came with eating a lifetime New York waterway fish.

Ma scampered around the apartment with the phone stuck mercilessly to her ear. Her voice was alive and her words came very quickly. He knew Ma was still okay. It was three years ago his doctor told him to be on the lookout for symptoms as the mercury in his blood was dangerously high. Earl hated his doctor. When the doctor told him to stop eating the fish he was catching, he hated him even more. Since he could remember best, he always ate his haul. He only shared the catch with his neighborhood friends and with Ma. There was always enough for a fish breakfast, lunch, and dinner, all to be washed down with seawater and scotch. *What's mercury but the* red crap *in a thermometer*, he thought. One evening after many scotches and fish, he went into Ma's medicine cabinet in the bathroom, took out the glass thermometer, broke it, and drank the red mercury. He wasn't sure how it tasted, but he was sure it only gave him a bellyache.

Perhaps, though, Ma wouldn't be so lucky. The guilt he felt was washed down his throat with another finger of scotch. The phone cord whizzed by the table with Ma following it.

"Okay, you go, Henrietta, you go, I'll call you if I hear more! Bye bye now." Ma untangled the cord from the kitchen chair, swung it back around the radiator, and hung the receiver back up. She sat back down next to Earl at the kitchen table.

"Earl, you haven't even touched the potatoes and vegetables!"

Earl burped silently in his mouth. "Aw, I don't want any more, Ma."

"The fish goes great with the vegetables, Earl. I am going to have so many leftovers, who's going to eat them?"

"You will, Ma."

He paused and watched as she bit another piece of fish.

"Ma, maybe you ought to lay off the fish. You eat my leftover vegetables and potatoes since you like 'em so much. Leave all the fish to me."

"No no, don't you worry. Maybe I'll bag them up and bring them to the church, then."

"Okay, Ma, I'll eat some. Right after I finish my drink."

The phone rang again. Ma leapt back to her feet and snatched the receiver off of the hook.

"Hello? Oh, Patty, what a day right? That fire and oh oh...."

Earl pushed his chair back and straightened his back up. There were two fingers of scotch left in the glass. Ma disappeared with the phone into the second room of the railroad apartment, closing the door behind her. Her voice was still strong but muffled now. *That was a relief,* he thought.

Earl didn't want to know any more about the goddamn fire; he heard every detail and conspiracy theory about the Himrod Street blaze for the last several hours. Two fingers of scotch would not be enough.

He stepped over the phone cord and made his way to the icebox and threw two ice cubes into the drink; instantly the liquid rose back up to looking like three fingers of scotch. Earl was pleased with his work. He shook the glass and sat back down at the table.

As he tuned out Ma and her reporting of the fire, he thought of the day gone by. *Fishing and the Lord; ain't nothing better than that,* he thought. That wasn't all he thought, however; he had spun some crazy yarns earlier in the day and especially with Tina.

Tina liked all-out fabrications rather than any part of the actual truth. Earl laughed to himself. One time, when they had first gone out fishing together, he convinced her that Jaws was a real shark and that Quint was a real fisherman that used to live on Cypress Avenue before his untimely death in Jaws's belly. Oh, she loved that one. After Earl found out she went searching the neighborhood for Quint's family, he gave her a fake phone number for Chief Brody and told her to give any family member she came across his number as there is a substantial life insurance policy that they were to inherit. Plus, he added, there was a cash reward for the person who gave them that number. Tina decided that she would extort the family once she found them with the knowledge of the insurance policy money and Chief Brody's number. Then she'd retire to the Seychelles.

Earl laughed to himself again and sucked on the scotch. Nope, she's still searching here on Cypress Avenue.

When he brought the glass back down to the table, something else had come back to him.

After the first bottle of scotch was emptied and thrown into the sea, Tina was grating on Earl with her stories about the girl she was in love with that just didn't love her and the guys on the street where she lived that catcalled to her every time she walked by, even though they knew she had no interest in them. Scotch and the sea can block that kind of whiney drone out only so much until one is forced to drown it out completely with some of their own meaningless anecdotal fictitious filler. Although this time, Earl wasn't sure if what he told Tina was completely untrue.

Ma came rolling back through to the front of the apartment, the cord dragging across everything as she went.

"Oh, and they said what? Oh, a woman fled the scene,
too. Who? Betty? I don't know anybody over there I will
have to ask my Earl about her. Yeah, he is home and not
eating his vegetables that I will have to give to the church."

"Ma, I'll eat them. I am not done with my drink yet."

Ma stabbed her fork in some more potato and waved it
in the direction of Earl as he spoke.

Earl put his head down and sipped the scotch. He felt a
little bit of relief now that she was off the fish and onto the
potatoes. Ma's phone call continued.

"Oh, and what? They think there was a young girl
found? Oh my god, well, you know that was an everyday
horror show over there, with all those young girls hanging
around the stoop. He did? Father John White? Well, I can
only hope his prayers send all their immortal souls straight
to heaven, Amen."

"Amen, Ma," said Earl.

She waved the fork with the potato on it back at him and
pointed to the uneaten vegetables on his plate. Earl smiled
and showed her his scotch. Ma waved the fork again, bit on
the potato, and shook her head before pulling the phone
cord and disappearing again into the back of the apartment.

Another sip of scotch made its way down into his gut.
Earl thought about what Ma was saying on the phone; the
young girl found dead in the fire. Also Father John's name,
always a byword among the son of a bitches in the neighborhood—but Earl never had the nerve to tell Ma. Even though
he knew it to be true, he almost didn't want to believe that

preachers could be capable of any type of sin or evil; there was a standard they chose to be held to and that standard could not be judged by man. It would be judged by the Lord. And Ma would never believe that men of the cloth even took shits, let alone would be involved in anything dirty in the neighborhood. A conversation like that would only turn into hours of aggravation and a marathon of Leroy Jenkins ministries for Earl. It was better to keep close to the scotch, scripture, and narrative of the church.

But only Ma was capable of keeping Earl in line. Not Goldie, not Tina, not the knob shiner down Fresh Pond Road; only Ma.

Earl's cousin Gerry was a born-again Christian, former Shriner who fancied himself a preacher. He answered everything with a generic praise to God that really carried no value or thought when he said it. It was just "hallelujah this" and "praise God that." When he found out Earl liked to fish, he repeatedly told the parable of Jesus and the five loaves and two fish whenever he was around. At first Earl found it amusing—even insightful—but not realistic. Earl had fished for many years and could eat three or four stripers by himself in one sitting and not feel full. He also didn't care for bread. What if those Jesus was feeding ate and felt the same way? Surely this kind of moral story held little to no merit in reality. But Gerry, now Pastor Gerry, made sure he told the tale every time he and Earl were in the same vicinity. Finally Earl'd had enough and suggested that Pastor Gerry put a lid on the fish parable and reinforced his suggestion with a fillet knife pressed against his gut. The parable of the fish and bread went back to the parable pile after that day. The two didn't speak for almost a year.

Then, earlier this month on one early Sunday morning or very late Saturday night, Earl was tying his fishing poles together and icing the scotch before he was to be on his way for some pier, for pole-fishing off the Rockaway Memorial Bridge. Usually Earl would be joined only by his fish bait, but he found Pastor Gerry on the stoop that morning with a bottle of gin. After some begging and half-crying, Earl allowed Gerry to tag along and being that it was Sunday, or very late Saturday (whichever you prefer), he thought it okay as long as Gerry carried the scotch cooler. The walk to the train and the train was a long and quiet process; Gerry stuck with his gin and Earl stuck with his poles. It was when they got off the A train and set up on the bridge, the sun just starting to crack a yellow into the midnight blue of dawn, that Pastor Gerry began to preach. At first Earl paid no attention to him; Pastor Gerry was yelling passages of scripture out into the hard-blowing sea spray. The surrounding fisherman couldn't make out a word he said and neither could Earl. The lines baited and the scotch in the red plastic cup poured, Earl relaxed and waited for the fishies.

In short order, Pastor Gerry figured out that no one could hear him and also that no one had cared to hear him. He sat down on top of the scotch cooler and watched Earl tug at the line, his fingers feeling for any nibble on the bait. Next to the cooler sat the white-and-green plaster bucket (now turned into a bona fide fish bucket). Two fish squirmed in the ocean water at the bucket's bottom. They were pretty good sized, enough to fetch a few bucks from a local seafood trader who needed to pad his haul. Earl never sold his catch; he would be taking these and any others he caught to Ma's cooking basin. The tide brought the fish in and Earl hoisted three more keepers into the fish bucket. Now with the five, Earl sucked down the scotch quickly as he had half his desired haul for the day. When the sun started to catch the sky on fire, Pastor Gerry sipped on his gin and began his descent.

"Praise God, Earl! Another morning is upon us, yes, praise God."

Earl nodded.

"What is better than being a harvester of the Lord in spirit and sea, right, Amen? You already know most of Jesus's disciples and his Apostles were fisherman, and they too followed our savior from shores of the Holy Land to the desert and back again. Amen."

The line and hook Earl yanked up contained no fish. He rebaited the line and drained what was left of the scotch. Before he cast, Pastor Gerry grabbed his arm.

"Earl, you have five fish here in this bucket. Do you know the parable of the five fish and the two loaves of bread? Hallelujah."

Earl pointed to the scotch cooler; it meant Pastor Gerry was to get up. He opened up the cooler and refilled his cup, closed the scotch and plopped a handful of ice in the drink. The scotch splashed a bit over the sides of the cup and onto his sea-cracked hands. Earl rubbed the scotch spray into his pants leg.

"That is the story of the two fish and five loaves of bread. You have it backwards."

Gerry was in the middle of taking down the gin when he answered. "No, no, it's a parable and there five fish not two. Bless you! Hallelujah."

"You kidding me, Gerry?"

"About the teachings of Jesus? No, I do not. Five fish, some bread. Praise God." His liter of gin was drawing to a close. So was Earl's patience.

"That's wrong, you dope. And what did I tell you about that story the last time? I don't want to hear it and I especially don't want to hear it if you can't even tell the damn thing right."

Pastor Gerry kicked the cooler and pounded the railing of the Rockaway Memorial Bridge. He pointed his fingers at Earl.

"Maybe you're wrong, Earl, you ever think that? I am the voice of God here. I studied the scripture! I know the parables by heart! There were five loaves and five fish! Praise God!" Pastor Gerry drained the rest of his gin and threw the empty plastic bottle into the salt water below.

Earl cast his line and looked Pastor Gerry over. "You look like you're finished with your drink. Good. Now, why don't you get the hell out of here, ya dope?"

Gerry wavered back and forth, his balance broken by the gin and the sea air blowing in from the east; the same place the sun was showing its face. He put his hands on his hips and faced Earl in an act of defiance.

"Why don't you get me out of here, you bottom feeder! Ya dope!"

That was all it took.

In an instant, Earl tossed his pole and clotheslined Pastor Gerry over the side of the Rockaway Memorial Bridge. The body hit the water and vanished into the deep.

BBBBBBBBBRRRRRRRRRRRIIIINNNNNNNG

The phone ringing woke Earl out of his daydream. Ma was standing over him with a fork full of potato and fish.

"Earl, the phone, it's Aunt Sandy. She says she hasn't heard from Gerry in a few weeks. She's worried. Would you take it?"

Earl looked at the phone and the fish on Ma's fork. Cousin Gerry and the mercury doctor flashed again into his mind. There was nothing he could do to change anything he had done.

The glass tumbler was just half-melted ice cubes and scotch water now. Next to it, the full plate of vegetables stared up at him.

Waste not, want not, he thought. Earl pushed the tumbler glass away and grabbed a fork.

"I'm about to eat my vegetables, Ma. I'll call her back later."

"Sandy, he'll call you back. Okay, okay, yes I'll pray for him. You too. Bye bye now." Ma dropped the receiver down and bit again into the fish.

"Fish came out great, son, just great. It's all God's doing! Amen."

"Amen, Ma," said Earl through the soft chew of potato.

The rain, the smoke, the phone, the mercury poisoning, and the waving fork all continued into the night.

PART 4

Nunny's III

Keith hurriedly dragged down the iron security gate that covered the windows of the store. It crashed and rattled against the concrete. Covered in multi-colored graffiti now, Keith took to looking over it every night for new paint before bolting the locks shut. Tonight was only a quick once over; even under the store awning the rain was getting to him in sprays sticking to his clothes. Not noticing anything new, he checked to make sure the locks were secure and reentered Nunny's.

Back inside, Dave had popped the cork on the final bottle of champagne and poured out three plastic Dixie cups full. The music was still going, but not for long; the final song on Slayer's *Hell Awaits*, his go-to end-of-the-night album, took its final measure in the speakers. As the drums and guitar-shredding faded, they were overtaken by snoring. That snoring belonged to Goldie. She had been slumped in the same chair all day, her hand still wrapped around an empty glass. Dave reached down and delicately slid the glass out of her hand and placed it in the sink; he knew the time was coming for him to wake her up and politely ask her to go home, but that would be put off until he and Keith were about to turn out the lights.

At the counter, Jim Douglas fiddled with the fishbowl full of vodka nips. He picked one up, examined it, and placed it back in the bowl. The battle of whether or not he really needed another one had been waged for the last half hour. Dave saw this and slid the champagne in front of him. Jim looked down at his dog.

"Well, Tabitha, one more for the road and then you and me go home. Sound okay, girl?" Tabitha darted her eyes around at the sound of his voice and then sighed through her nose. She was full of Milk-Bones and wanted nothing more than to shut her eyes for a good long time. It was the thing that most men full of bubbles wanted, too. Man's best friend and man's best mirror.

Dave reached down and pet Tabitha across the head. She closed her eyes after each pass of his hand.

When his hand reached further down across the neck and onto the belly, Tabitha's leg shook rhythmically. When Dave slowed, the leg slowed; when he sped up, the leg sped up. When he stopped, the dog just stared at him.

"She's such a good pup, Jim."

Jim pulled his hand out of the vodka fishbowl quickly and tapped his fingers on the counter.

"Yes, well, she is a thirteen-year-old pup."

Dave rubbed her a little more, this time noticing a mass under her skin on her belly. The dog's legs stopped when he touched there and she sighed again. Dave had a dog like Tabitha years ago and knew what those masses meant. All one could do is give them a lot of Milk-Bones, plenty of table scraps, and rubs until there was no more time to give them. Jim had stopped giving rubs to Tabitha. He just couldn't accept the masses on her belly, so he let others comfort the old girl.

Jim watched Dave petting Tabitha. His hand went back into the vodka fishbowl and he produced two nips, set them on the counter, and unscrewed the blue caps.

"That dog and I have walked around every inch of this neighborhood. I haven't been with another living thing as much as I have been with her."

Dave smiled and continued petting the dog.

"And I'll tell you this," Jim picked up the open vodka nips close to his face, "When she's gone, I will miss Tabitha girl more than I would miss any lady. That's right. More than my wife, my mistress, my mother, even the first pretty virgin I ever stuck my business in. Tabitha is my only girl." He finished the nips and tossed them in the garbage.

Dave nodded. He knew just what he meant. Keith returned from the rain, grabbed his plastic Dixie cup, and pointed to Goldie. It was finally closing time.

"We need to wake this one up and get her home." Dave sighed in agreement and stood up to turn off the stereo and kitchen lights.

"Keith, we still going to the bar?"

As he softly shook Goldie he answered, "After everything that happened on this avenue, let alone this neighborhood today? Hell, yes. Hell yes, we are." Dave checked his watch.

"Well, it's getting really late, man; we should leave now. It's a fifteen-minute walk without the rain."

Keith looked down at Goldie. She was completely coma-tose. He watched her for a moment; her blonde hair was

matted and haggard, her fingernails dirty, her teeth bad—
but he imagined her fifty years ago. It was all there: the hair
was golden and soft; the hands manicured and tended to
each evening before bed; the teeth where they were supposed
to be—all the trimmings of a neighborhood pinup girl. He
felt a sadness for her right then; not a sadness of loss, but
of what is now. *Age wasn't any good to anyone,* he thought. It
had been exceptionally shitty to Goldie, self-made or not.

Keith reached behind the bar and took out a small
blanket. He draped it over Goldie, smoothed her hair, and
shut off the remaining light switches. Dave laughed.

"We going to leave her here in the store?"

Keith shrugged.

"With all the liquor?"

Keith shrugged again. "Let's just get to the bar. Jim,
you coming?

Jim was weaving back and forth a bit, nothing new for
him. He finished the champagne and kneeled down on the
green and white tile next to Tabitha. "Come on, old girl;
let's make it one more walk tonight before we head home."

Tabitha stood up and looked out into the street through
the glass front door of Nunny's. She put her head down and
sighed through her nose.

PART 5

she calls herself betty

at the top of St. Aloysius's steps, Betty watched the rain sheet and bounce off the gray slate that made up the walkway of the church. It was an old church, born in need, kept up in necessity. Most days the church was empty; Father John told Betty once that the congregation had turned coagulated. He wasn't far off, by the looks of it; those who did come around were the same sordid group that spent most of their time near the tabernacle and all their tax return money at the track. Next to the church sat an empty parking lot; on the days it wasn't empty, kids would find their way there after school hours to sneak tall cans of suds or to smoke laced spliffs. The weddings and funerals declined over the years as patrons opted to pass their loved ones into a fire and ash instead of a mass and burial. The kids of those who put offerings in every Sunday didn't go to church and so, in turn, neither would their children. The cycle produced less and less of a return in people and pennies, and the business of the Church was becoming a full-fledged begging operation—more than it ever had been in the past. Yet still the doors stayed open, the fifteen hold-outs kept showing up, and Father John kept on his neighborhood crusade.

St. Aloysius was just as Betty had remembered it, but now less necessary.

A navy blue Mercedes LX pulled up in front of the church steps and waited. Betty coughed before descending the church steps and entered the car. The white leather inside was fresh and cold.

Betty maneuvered her neck around as she buckled her seat belt and gave the inside a once over; the car appeared to be factory-new. The scent of coconut immediately hit her nose and lips as Father John sped away from the church. He made it three traffic lights before speaking to her.

"Is this the last time I will be seeing you?"

Betty nodded.

"Well?"

"Yes."

"So you are going to say goodbye to Zogby's stoop, and leave for good?"

Betty didn't answer.

"Where will you go?"

"West."

"West? What is there for you?"

"Just west."

Father John nodded and opened both his and the passenger windows all the way down. Instantly the air and rain blasted, loudly yelling and splashing between them as the car roared through the Ridgewood streets. It lasted forever in Betty's mind but really only seconds slipped by;

with a flick of the chrome button on the door panel, the windows made their way back on up again. Betty's hair was now in her face and stuck in her mouth. Father John laughed.

"Like that?"

"What the hell did you do that for?"

"I always air out the car; especially when I smell bullshit."

Betty looked at Father John through wet hair.

"It's fucking pouring."

"It's holy water, baby."

The half-orange, half-white fluorescent light coming from the street lamps reflected the rain on the windshield and across Betty's face.

"Holy water my ass." Betty wiped the rainwater off her clothes and onto the floor mats in disgust. Father John smirked and continued driving. He didn't mind soaking the floor mats at all because it wasn't his car; it was the monsignor's Mercedes. He spilled scotch and suds and massaged them with his foot into the floor mats driving from one end of Ridgewood to the other in that thing—a little rain water would do no harm. The monsignor was a tired, dimwitted old man who once left his car keys in the confessional. Why he had them there in the first place Father John never knew, but when he found them and took the Mercedes for a run, he never gave them back. These days, he'd wait until the old bastard headed to his room for bed, usually right after Jeopardy, and he'd disappear with the car to help the sinners of Cypress Avenue.

Father John kept his eyes ahead as the drive continued, but spoke through the windshield wipers squeak.

"Listen, Betty, sugar. We only have three more blocks. Let's just say our goodbyes as adults."

Mostly dry now, Betty nodded. Father John pushed off the gas pedal and pulled in next to a Johnny pump.

"Understand that I always wanted you to say goodbye to Zogby."

She nodded again.

"You see…" Father John paused, waving his hand around in the air as he spoke. "We just never got around to doing it. But it's here with a healthy, open heart that I take you to him. Look there."

Up ahead, the yellow tape that cordoned off the street was half-guarded by two policemen in a patrol car. Both officers sat in the front seat with their heads down; their faces awash in green police radio light glow. Father John followed the glow and stalled the car right ahead of theirs. Neither officer stirred.

"How funny; you didn't even need me. Those cops aren't even awake…." his voice trailed off.

Betty had already unlocked the door and was pushing her away onto the sidewalk.

Father John grabbed her arm made it out of the door. "It wasn't supposed to end this way."

Betty maneuvered her arm free of his grasp and spit as hard as she could in his face. It splattered on his coat and coated the rearview mirror in a spray. She waited for a moment as the preacher blinked his eyes to remove the mucus-heavy saliva from where it had lodged under his eye.

"This is the way it ends for us, Father."

He didn't respond but stared straight ahead in the darkness and falling rain. Betty nodded, exited the Mercedes, and shut the door with her foot.

The spit cleared from his eyes, Father John watched Betty as she made her way through the police tape and the raindrops to the bottom stair of Zogby's stoop. She left the car without an umbrella and embraced the sheeting rain. *Holy water,* he thought to himself. *Perfect holy water.* Perhaps he, too, should go out and get into that holy rain to cleanse whatever was left of his life. The day's events seemed to dictate that as the only response: Zogby's suicide, Ms. Madre blowing up her building and little Sarah Jane, and now Betty standing in the rain of a blood-stained stoop. His role in all of this was clear.

In his jacket pocket, standing guard over his heart, was a cold flask of Southern scotch. Perhaps that was the only saving he could only receive this night. He produced it from his pocket and unscrewed the top; the spiced scotch scent slipped out and huddled under his nose. Its scent was home; his momma at the stove stirring the pot, his father in his robe and slippers with a coffee mug full of the same spiced scotch for breakfast, Skippy the dog wagging his tail at the prospect of a leash and a walk into the great backyard near the weeping willow tree. His father would bellyache before taking the dog out for a poop, but not when he had the spiced-scotch mug filled. After the mug was drained it was refilled more than before. He'd then leash the dog and grab young Father John by the collar so he would follow him out the door and onto the great expanse of a green lawn that his grandfather seeded when they first moved into the house.

There he would let Skippy do what dogs do and share the mug with his twelve-year-old son. As the morning breeze made its presence known, he would tell young Father John about bad seeds and how planting them never grew good roots. Pointing across the lawn to a group of three trees, his father said that two of them were fine, but one would eventually have to come down—but as long as they had their mug full of scotch that could wait. Skippy died two years later and was buried under the bad tree. Six months later, the tree died and fell over.

Father John sipped deep as his mind wandered further on the back of the spiced scent: His face was all smiles as he sat in his first car, a yellow Pontiac LeMans, and pressed the gas pedal as far as it could go down the back road that wrapped around his childhood home. No one ever drove their cars that way; it was an unofficial private road for the Whites. Young Father John kept his foot on the pedal and the LeMans soared past overhanging flora and low tree branches while kicking up the sundried dirt of the road into a low cloud behind the taillights. He had the mug of scotch next to him in the car; it splashed over the side and dotted the black interior with spiced spots. Father John pressed the pedal down further and drove straight hard into the glare of the sun, summer birds sailing overhead, the weeping willow tree continuing its weep on the White's land. The dust cloud engulfed the car and yellowed the window so much that by the time he saw the bikes with the two young girls coming towards him, it all turned into a dream. After it all happened, he left the scene and ran back to the house. There he buried the mug and the spiced rum next to Skippy and the fallen, bad-root tree. After the judge ruled it a very unfortunate accident, John left the estate and found Jesus. He never left the scotch.

The gas tank of the monsignor's Mercedes hovered around empty, just where Father John liked it to be. He had no intention of filling it back up. The old bastard wouldn't remember where the gas line was the last time he drove it anyway. Whatever was left would go to the foot driving down on the pedal. He sipped the flask, the scotch shot down his throat, and he sped off, screeching down the street as he went. The police instantly picked up their heads and started the car, taking after the fleeing Mercedes.

Betty hadn't noticed any of it; her eyes had been fixed on the gray of the stoop and the spot she imagined Zogby always spent his days. Under her foot she noticed blood stains and next to that, a beer can. Both must've belonged to him. Descending to bended knees, she picked up the can and sniffed the opening for the familiar smell of Kent cigarettes. It wasn't there. A little beer clung to life in the can and after a pause, Betty drank it down. In the warm, stale suds she found the Kents and the taste of Zogby. The familiar rush of saltwater fishing and clam shacks filled her sinuses. Slurping down clams and wiggling toes in sun-warmed sand, that's the way they were. She laughed and smoothed her hand across the bottom stair, frowning, as she fought back the coming tears. Now all they had was a gray-painted, bloody stoop.

She pressed her cheeks close to the middle step of the stoop. This is where he would sit and smoke and sip and stare down the length of Cypress Avenue. Her arms reached out across the concrete step and she laid her hand palm down on top of it. In one stroke she smoothed across the wetness and roughness and thought of Zogby's unshaven cheekbones and scruffy, pointed chin. Many a morning she would hold that stubbly face close under the hot, blasting water of the showerhead in silence. Just Zogby, she, the steam, and the shower curtain, wrapped in this morning ritual. There was no world. There was no why. There was only a porcelain tub with green-tiled walls and unpolished chrome shower knobs.

Betty reached out to the rain-wet stoop railing and felt it slip beneath her fingertips. She imagined it was Zogby's arms around her in their morning shower, sliding across the lower arch of her back above the tailbone and then up to her elbows and down to her small wrists. There he would grab her hands and hold tight to not lose grip as the Ivory soap lather bubbled between every crevice of their bodies. There they would stay until the hot water tank gave them the last bit of warmed water it had left. The knobs would turn off in one squeak to the right. A few drops would seep from the shower head and dot their toes as they both held in embrace. The soap gone and the steam dissipating away, their morning shower had washed them and the outside world away.

Back on the stoop, she squinted through wet eyelashes down at the gray painted cement steps to see the bloodstains. She smoothed her fingers across the stain and the rain slowed. She began to speak.

"Benjamin. Can you hear me? I'm here. I am here. You bum, you went and did it without me. And of course it's my fault, it always was. Go ahead and say it. Or I'll say it all for you, ya bum. This is who I am. I ran instead of stayed. I hid instead of faced. I watched from the sidelines instead of raced back to your side and explained myself."

Before she said another word, she looked herself over and brought her hands to her face. She spoke through trembling lips and soaked fingertips.

"Ben. Ben, I have to say this to you, and I have had to say it for some time now. Okay? Let me just get it out. Back when it was you and me, I was a foolish girl; a foolish girl with a man who kept his head in the sand alongside those clams we so loved. It was so warm in that sand and you were so warm to me, I didn't know what to do with any of it but go with the summer days and spend my time with you and that warmth, until another man turned his warmth towards me. I didn't know what to do with that, either, except embrace it and hurt you and myself. And then I just couldn't stop. I lived on the beach with you among the sand and clam shacks and the streets and high rises with him. I loved them both Ben, I didn't mean to, but both the tar streets and the golden sand, I loved them both. I loved the summer burn that made the tar sticky and the sand too hot to walk on. I walked both of those roads at the same time and I couldn't stop myself, I swear I tried."

The rain became a slow drizzle and the street became still around her. Betty moved her hand from her face back to the bloodstain and shivered as she touched it.

"That day on the beach when I knew you figured it all out and I saw the look on your face, I ran as far as I could down Crossbay Boulevard, and when I couldn't run anymore, I got on the next bus and took it as far as it would take me. That was all I could do. What a complete asshole, right? That was my solution. Disappear on a bus and don't look back."

A loud roll of thunder echoed across the sky and off the apartment buildings. Betty waited for the lightning, but it never came. A gust of wind did come, however, and with it a dull gong of church bell. She continued her confession to Zogby in the darkness.

"When I moved back here and learned that everyone was gone…and now, you are gone, and all that's left was me continuing on, unable to face a goddamn thing, I hoped that time and chance would do what I could not do."

Betty began to sob with her head close again to the middle stoop step.

"In that I was right, Ben. Time and chance made our beds and took you away. And so here I am now, left only with a bloodstain and an empty beer of you to say I am sorry to. If there is a sorry and sorrow enough I can leave here with you, or if my life could be traded for yours, I would. I would do so now with an open, clear heart. I always wanted the sand over the streets, Ben. I always wanted you."

Instead of more lightning and thunder, airbrakes shrieked and squealed as a rush of air and water washed over the curb. It was the bus. The doors opened.

"Lady, you all right? Why don't you get in? This is the last one until dawn."

Betty looked up at the bus; it wasn't lit up at all and the entrance was completely dark, making the face behind the voice obscured. The rain had once again picked up and she started to notice the cod in her feet. The bus driver beeped the horn.

"Lady, hello? It has to be now."

She smoothed her hand once more over the middle stair of the stoop, picked herself up, and called out to the operator.

"Where does this bus go?"

"Down Crossbay Boulevard. Last stop is Rockaway Beach. You headed that way?"

Betty nodded. "Could you let me off on Crossbay, right near Kenneth Wayne's Bait and Tackle?"

"Fine, fine, but it has to be now."

She picked up the beer can and cradled it close to her face. They would go together away from the stoop and Cypress Avenue.

The bus, the barnacles, the beach, Ben Zogby, and Betty it would be.

The bus operator waived the fare and closed the doors.

"Lady, do you live in that building?"

"No."

"Oh. Yeah, some bad stuff went down earlier today."

"Bad stuff always happens on Cypress Avenue."

"I know exactly what you mean. I saw a lady fall on her face this morning running after this very bus. Of course, I wasn't driving it, but I was at the deli up the block and saw the whole thing."

"That's nice," Betty looked away and slumped into a seat behind the operator's chair. She closed her eyes, smiled, and began whispering to the empty beer can. The faint scent of stale beer and cigarettes would stay with her now.

The driver shrugged and turned the big black wheel, righted the bus, and sent it hurtling down Cypress Avenue. As the wheels splashed and sloshed through the storm puddles, he raised the volume on his portable radio and went back to listening to the distorted AM radio voices talking through the tiny speaker.

Presently, the bells of St. Aloysius rang the half hour mark. Thirty minutes to midnight.

the slow midnight

the Blue Collar Transient Passerby Bum Bar was quiet except for the heat hissing out of the pipes. Mid-July and the heat was somehow still on. Usually it was an accepted fact that it would be on and those who couldn't take the heat spent their time on the back porch, but this day had been unbearably muggy and warm. Sam Jean knocked on the wood of the countertop and got the attention of the bartender.

"Hey, what is this horseshit? Do you really need the heat on?"

The bartender sauntered over and smiled at Sam. He was dressed in his usual black sports jacket and dark red shirt; his face sporting a handlebar moustache with a hint of a growing goatee coating the point of his chin. He produced a comb from his back pocket and ran it through his slicked-back black hair; a custom he always performed between pours and rings of the register. Some called him Cloot, some nothing at all, but he was always there among the beer caps and bar rags.

"The heat is always on in here, unfortunately, Mister Jean. You know that."

Sam sighed and looked at Dezzy. Without making eye contact, she laughed under her breath. Mr. Jean did not.

"Well, it just seems like a deadhead thing to have the heat coming up on a day like this. This day has been bad enough for everyone, between the summer heat and all the happenings in the neighborhood. Could you crack a window or something?"

Cloot produced another glass and filled it with Sam's choice red wine. He grasped the stem and slid the glass in front of him.

"Afraid that wouldn't help much. Why not have another drink? That should help. On the house." He ran the comb through his hair again and smiled.

Sam shrugged and looked around the bar. The leftovers, the finalists for closing the bar down tonight, all congregated in one corner: Dezzy, Keith, Dave, Tina, and Jim sat together, lining the length of the countertop. They all had been quiet for the most part. Tabitha snoozed beneath the bar stool.

"Do we know when Zogby's wake will be?" asked Keith.

"Well, what Tabitha and I heard from Fran before we met you at Nunny's is that Father John White will be setting all of that up. It has to be by Wednesday, right?" Tabitha picked her head up when she heard her name but quickly set it back down and sighed through her nose.

"Yes. That sounds right. The funeral will probably will be held at St. Aloysius. I don't think I'll go," said Sam.

"Me either," echoed Dezzy.

Sam sipped his wine and continued. "It will just be another shit show with that Father John White."

Everyone nodded in agreement and took a drink. By the time they were done, Cloot appeared again and ran the bar rag along the length of the countertop, picking up their glasses and wiping underneath them as he went. Their drinks were almost empty. Dave drummed his hands on his thighs and turned to Keith.

"Can you remember a day like this, though?"

"Nope. Not me."

A car raced by down Cypress Avenue followed by blue and red flashing lights. Not one of them flinched.

"It's like all of a sudden this avenue is cursed. The things that went wrong today never go wrong over the course of one day all together; unless it's the end of the world, maybe."

Sam laughed. "We'd be so lucky if it were the end of the world."

"I'm just saying. I'm forty-three years old. I've seen a lot of crap go down around this neighborhood; hell, Keith and I caused some of it!"

Keith nodded. "Yes, we did."

Dave patted him on the arm and continued. "But nothing ever like this. I can't make sense of it. Christ, old Goldie is asleep, locked inside Nunny's right now!"

Everyone laughed. Sam shook his head.

"It's Faustian." The group turned and looked at Dezzy. She was staring at her reflection in her cup of wine. Cloot looked at her as well and listened from the far side of the bar.

"It's what?" asked Dave.

"Faustian. Faust. It's a poem by Goethe called 'Faust.' The poem is a pact made with the devil gone wrong. Maybe that's what this all is."

"The devil indeed," Sam grunted and checked his watch. It was ten minutes to midnight.

"In the poem it takes twenty-four years for their pact to run out, one year for the twenty-four hours in a day. But maybe, here, it was just twenty-four hours, one day—this Sunday. Look, it's almost midnight."

Keith looked at Dave. "What, are we telling ghost stories now? It's just been a bad, well, really bad day, that's all."

"Haven't you guys ever felt like this neighborhood is damned? The way we are, the way we live. Nobody notices us; nobody cares about our comings or goings but us. The cars that drive through this neighborhood never stop, they just pass on through. The buses sometimes don't even stop. No one visits and no one wants to be here, but yet we all remain. We all live day-to-day, check-to-check, in sorrow, behind the bottle and the drugs, and even knowing all of this, none of us ever leaves. It's almost as if we are trapped here. Maybe Mister Zogby figured it out and knew the only way off this avenue was…."

Sam slowly put his hand up and covered Dezzy's mouth. "Dezzy, baby, stop now."

She pushed his hand away and shook her head. "No, I am telling you, this is a deal with the devil gone wrong. And no amount of praying at St. Aloysius is going to change any of it, for any of us."

Keith kicked his chair back, stood up, and saluted the bar.

"Well, as long as I have my booze and Nunny's, I'll stay in hell."

Jim and Dave stood up as well and the three of them clanked their glasses together.

"To hell!" said Keith.

"To the devil!" shouted Dave.

"Amen!" laughed Jim.

Tabitha picked her head up again during the commotion. Once it was over she was back asleep, her head resting on her paws.

Sam drained his wine as well. When he turned to Dezzy, her head was back down, staring at her reflection in the glass. What she saw in that reflection, Sam didn't ask.

As the glasses were drained, the sound of police sirens echoed outside; they grew loud and raced passed the bar. Then they were gone. The bar became silent. The hope was the police sirens were not responding to anything else on Cypress Avenue or even in Ridgewood. The possibility that they were, though, hung over the room like the early so many mornings before.

Littered along the countertop was a half-full crop of their favorite suds, swill, and bubbles. Cloot spied the group's empty glasses and their quiet and sauntered back towards them.

"I have an announcement. You have all been through so much today, and in honor and memory of Mister Zogby I've decided to keep the bar open for the remainder of the night. And drinks are on me. What do you all say?"

That livened up the men and brought their silence into a cheer and a wave of high fives. Dezzy banged her wine glass on the bar counter in agreement until the stem broke, sending shards of the fake crystal in almost every direction. The room erupted in laughter. It was decided there would be no need to go home tonight. There was no need to go anywhere, because there was nowhere to go. They all were right where they had to be. They had been all along and in that, they would remain.

The church bells became their song, belling until midnight.

Cloot floated by each of their empty glasses and freshened them up with a grace and ease that was almost undetectable. Upon the last pour he combed his hair back and spoke, his voice lulling them back into their now full cups.

> "How the breath is heavy with the dew of
> downtown
> Right before the Heavens open up and spill
> their swill on the
> Passerby
> Transients
> Worked to the bone
> Blue collar blokes
> Of this fine town
> How the eyes sink back into their holes—dark
> and true
> Right as the J train slides its shaft into Virginia
> Station
> And those summer swans in belly-baring
> t-shirts and sundresses

Bite their lower lips, fix their hair, and
    straighten out their spines so it sits just
    right—
They are, that which we,
The transient, blue-collar, bone-driven bums
    of Brooklyn/Queens have to dream upon;
Post pub action—
Prior to squalls and storms overflowing the
    sewers—
As the cars run out of gasoline—
As the dime runs out on the pay phone and
    change is looser to find than gold bullion—
How my words become far and few between
    my bride and my mother—
My father and I never spoke unless the game
    was on the television,
Or we passed a few Rheingold's between us,
Right as dusk slipped into twilight and the
    blues, grays, reds, golds, purples, yellows—
    all pastels
Blended into one super shade of color and set
    down over the sky above my home
Yours too, baby—
That hue was the time we used to meet,
Foot of the Kosciusko Bridge next to the still
    of the Newtown Creek
You'd say we'd meet on the division
    line—Brooklyn/Queens
And the polluted creek was good enough for a
    swim—

Blue collar transient passerby bums
You and I
And all this horseshit between us
But now my breath is heavy with the dew of
    downtown—
Lucifer star set high above the sorrowed
    midnight
Where Sam and Dezzy continued their dance
Goldie fast asleep among sealed bottles of
    booze
Keith and Dave dying on delivery day
Corporal Benjamin Zogby reunited with Betty
Father John White headed to that red night
The ghost of Pat Wilson's son still slithering
    up the fire escape
And Earl still feeding his Ma that fish full of
    mercury
My dear Ms. Madre called home
Sending Ivan the Russian straight there too
With two little ladies finding their way from
    the seventh circle of hell
Because I know they will be back someday
    soon
To the sidewalks and side streets of Cypress
    Avenue."

END

ACKNOWLEDGMENTS

this book could not have been possible without the love, guidance, and support of the following people:

To my best friend and wife, Audrey Anne and our beautiful Alice Jane. Thank you for loving and supporting me during this journey—I love you both more than life.

To my amazing and beautiful kids, Johnny and Della—I am blessed you are mine and love you both to space and back.

Endless love to my family: Mom, Dad, Chris and Nicole Figliola, Aunt Rosie, Michelle and Lilly Parsinski, and the entire Figliola family. See you all at Sunday dinner.

To Mark "Foundries" Zustovich for years of friendship and life—I couldn't ask for a better friend or brother. Love you.

To Keith, Dave, and the Nunny's family for your encouragement, friendship, and the bubbles.

To the crew: Jason "Beaker" Peterla, Michael Heiss, Jack Tar, Mauro Dizon, Melton Sawyer, The great Al Randall, Rocco Dispirito, David Amram, the late Ken Siegelman, Anthony Vigorito and everyone at Brooklyn Poetry Outreach, Joe Bartlett, Terry Trahim, Jimmy A, Bayside/

Key West Dan, and everyone at Buckle up for Chi. Thank you for the laughs and friendship.

To my work family—thank you for all of the support you gave to me and the book. Love you all.

To Anthony Scaramucci for opening the door for me and being a friend.

To my agent Ian Kleinert for believing in me and my work.

To Anthony Ziccardi, Heather King, and everyone at Permuted Press for all your hard work and support. Thank you for taking a chance on me and the book. You made my dream come true. I am eternally grateful.

Thank you to music to which I could not exist without.

Finally, to you, the reader for picking up my book, thumbing through it, and making that choice to buy it. Happy reading. Thank you.

As the late great poet Robert Creeley once told me, ONWARD!

ABOUT THE AUTHOR

Mike Figliola is a writer, television/radio reporter, and producer who has called New York City—specifically Queens—his home for more than thirty years. He has written hundreds of poems and has read them on a regular basis at such venues as the famed Cornelia Street Café in NYC with actor John Ventimiglia and poet Frank Messina, and has been a featured poet in the Brooklyn Poet Laureate's "Brooklyn Poetry Outreach" in Park Slope Brooklyn. He has served as a producer, writer, and reporter in radio and TV on both local and national platforms.